PLAY (FETTERED #6)

Chloe & Eli

LILIA MOON

COPYRIGHT

Chapter One

CHLOE

I want to flop down in the big chair in the corner of my store, the one I use to keep nervous men from knocking into all our displays. But I know from past experience that the second I do that, a customer will walk in the door, and they expect the owner of Pretty Things to match her wares. Classy, sexy, and offering escape into a moment where nothing practical matters.

Clearly they've never run a business. However, inventory's finally done, my new orders are ready to head out the door, and I didn't strangle Mandy even once, for which I deserve chocolate and a martini. I wave at my perky assistant, dressed in her signature pink, which is a little dusty from digging through boxes in the back room. "Go home."

She looks moderately horrified. "It's not closing time yet."

She's still not entirely convinced I can handle the store without her. The fact that I did so for nearly ten years somehow isn't convincing. However, I didn't hire her to understand me—I hired her to fill in for my holes, the ones that have no patience left for fluttery brides and their overexcited mothers. I would pay Mandy's sizable salary, and gladly, for that alone, but she's also detail focused and never forgets a customer or her preferences, and in these four walls, those are worth their weight in gold. I pull a curvaceous water bottle out of my bag and point Mandy gently at the door. "Go. Let Brandon rub your feet."

That gets her moving. The man in her life is treasure and she knows it.

I take a seat on the stool behind the counter as she leaves and drink the water that will have to stand in for a martini until closing time. I hide a sigh as a tinkling chime announces a new arrival before I do much more than wet my lips. I manage a slightly frayed smiled at the young woman, blonde, gorgeous, and utterly self-confident, who has just entered. "Welcome to Pretty Things."

She takes her time scanning the store and then strides over to my counter. "Hi. I'm Ari, and I'm hoping you're Chloe."

She's younger than most of my clientele, and this is no bride wandering into an upscale lingerie boutique for the first time. "Yes, I'm Chloe."

Her smile could melt far harder walls than mine. "Perfect. Harlan said you would be easy to find."

My afternoon just got a lot more interesting. The big man with the tough-guy ink and soft eyes is one of my best customers—and the manager of the best kink club in town, so if I'm reading the light in the bright-blue eyes facing me right, an idea I've been noodling on and off over the past couple of months may have just come to me.

I grab a second stool and slide it around the counter. "You're from Fettered?"

She grins, and I'm looking at a younger version of me. "I am. I have a business proposal I want to discuss with you."

I know what the younger version of me would want to hear. "Good. If you hadn't come to me, I was planning on coming to you. I think half your membership has wandered through my shop recently."

I've said exactly the right thing. She's delighted, and young enough to show it. "You make really beautiful things, and our members are smart enough to appreciate quality."

That they are—and they show off their sexy underwear a lot more frequently than most of my clients. Which is why my brain's been noodling. "Tell me what you have in mind." I know my request is a bit of a test. I'm the last person to judge someone for being too young or too female to have good ideas, but I want to know who I'm dealing with. And I'm fascinated and pleased that Fettered has sent Ari in as their representative.

"We'd like to work with you to develop some styles more specifically suited for the kink lifestyle. With features like tie releases so that underwear can be removed from a restrained sub."

She's watching me carefully. The tests are going both ways. I give her what she needs. "Thank you for not assuming I'm too boring and vanilla to run with this. I got into this business out of my work designing theater costumes. You won't find shock or judgment here."

Her whole body warms. "I like you. Harlan said I would."

That's entirely mutual. "I appreciate him sending you to me."

I leave space, and she steps into it gracefully. "We want someone who can handle frank discussions of our needs and then turn them into something beautiful that will last through the abuse our members might put it through."

I laugh, because she's a deep pool of awesome and she clearly knows it. "Most of my designers and seamstresses also work in theater. Trust me, there's nothing you can do to lingerie that an actor can't do to their costume."

She grins at me. "Maybe don't tell the Doms that straight off. They might take it as a dare."

I laugh and look around my shop, because we're likely to get interrupted any minute, and I want to know more about this deal we're going to grow between us. "Were you hoping I could sell it here?"

Ari follows my eyes around the store and makes a wry face. "I don't think that's helpful for either of our brands."

My weeks of noodling crystalize around her words. It's time to find out just how deep into this a sex club is willing to go. "I could develop a line specifically for those with more kinky desires, but designing the pieces is only half the game here. We'd need the retail side too. An online presence, perhaps, but I'd strongly suggest a physical storefront as well. These items won't be inexpensive, and quality sells best when people can touch and feel."

She leans forward a little, and I catch a glimpse of very shrewd negotiator in her eager blue eyes. "We were thinking you could develop the line for Fettered. We'd sell it at the club. Nothing that needs to be staffed all the time, at least to start, but something like a portable shop that opens a couple of afternoons or evenings a month. In our lounge, maybe, where people can model for each other." She winks. "That will sell a lot more merchandise, trust me."

She's pitching with passion and interest and not a trace of nerves. I wonder if Fettered knows what they have in her. "Would you be representing the club's interests as we work out the details?"

She grins. "Yes. It was my idea, and I know how to keep the Doms I work for in line."

She gets bonus points for every part of that sentence, and so do they. Which is unfortunate, because it means she's not poachable. "Good. It sounds like you have a solid idea of what you want, and potentially a lot of people who would like to have some input. I'd like to get them engaged early on so the designs can fully reflect what they need and want, but I'd also like to define a small group, on your side and mine, who will be making the decisions."

It's a speech I've given before—herding theater people isn't for wimps.

She's nodding before I'm halfway finished. "Perfect. You'll have both. I'll handle sign-off from our decision-makers. As far as input, I can gather a group to talk to you, or, if you'd rather, you can come hang out in the lounge one night and observe and ask questions."

Test number two just landed. This bright-eyed woman doesn't give an inch, even when she's smiling, and I'll be smart to remember that. "Both. I'd like to visit your club, and I'd like to bring a few of my designers to a smaller meeting with some of your members. I'm thinking there might be some interest in special orders as well." Which will have my people drooling. They make the same thing more than once because I pay them very well to do it, but they adore creating things. They'll be all over this. I don't let the warm glow of that show—lovely as she is, Ari's the toughest negotiator I've faced in years. She doesn't need to know I'm a cupcake for my people.

Ari's eyes flash amused. "If you're willing to consider special orders, I hope you can handle a stampede."

We're going to get along very well. "We can. Is there anything else you want me to hear before someone walks in who wants the only shade of green panties I don't carry?"

She stands up from her stool, laughing. "Just one. Scorpio was wearing a gorgeous black silk corset last night. Please tell me you have that in blue."

I don't—but I will by tonight. And I think I might just pay a certain club a visit to deliver it.

Chapter Two

ELI

I tinker with the bells and whistles on my electronic keyboard, happy to be back making music in a place where loud and energetic is more appreciated than fancy technique. I joined the Seattle Symphony partly because they play things by people who aren't dead yet and partly for their less-demanding travel schedule, but they still swallow my life sometimes. Today, I've been spit back out, and spending the night as the keyboard guy and cello flunky for Doms on the Bottom is exactly my idea of a good time.

I nod at a couple of subs standing near the stage, clearly hoping for more than a polite smile, and go back to work. Scorpio wants to try Quint's new ballad tonight, and that requires a little more subtlety from my keyboard than our usual loud and enthusiastic. Which is fine by me. My job is to be the condiments on the burger, adding flavor and spice and doing my best not to get in the way of the overall experience.

Which tonight is going to include the delightful pleasure of watching the toughest Dom in the club squirm. I don't know how Scorpio found out that Quint writes music, or how she keeps digging it out of him, but she does. This one is soft and lush and obviously an ode to the woman in his life. I wink at Meghan, who's handing out drinks behind the bar.

She scans my groupies and snickers.

I shrug. In one form or another, they've always been there. At least at the club, there are rules. I got tired of random sex with random strangers a long time ago, and the subs I tend to enjoy playing with generally aren't the ones prepared to stand around and wait until I notice them.

I like spice on more than my burgers.

Jackson swings in behind his drums, setting down a bag that looks like it's visited more continents than I have, and pulls out his sticks. "Welcome back. No cello tonight?"

I considered it, but I need to step out of that skin for a while. "After this last week, my bow feels welded to my hand. Time for a break." The symphony is recording, and the new piece they commissioned is heavy on the low strings. Which is nothing to complain about, but it's kept the eight of us who play cello hopping busy.

Jackson picks up a hand drum and starts a gentle, intricate beat. Not what he'll be playing later tonight, but it's a nice way to get the blood flowing.

I glance over at my two groupies and shake my head. They haven't even noticed him. Jackson might be a baby Dom, but he's got a really interesting sense of presence. One I suspect a lot of subs will regret underestimating some day. "Has Quint kicked your ass out onto the floor yet?" Most trainees pull hard against the leash that Fettered's head trainer keeps them on, but Jackson seems content to play his drums and watch.

He gives me a shrug that manages to say nothing at all and amps up his beat. I take the hint and find a simple chord progression that matches wherever he's headed. It feels like something that might have blown in from a village in Tibet. Which is totally not what they pay us for, but given our basic

Dom predispositions, that never weighs on either of us overly much.

It also chases away my two fickle groupies. Apparently they're not looking for condiments.

I pick out a subtle melody line that weaves into Jackson's beat. It would sound better on the cello, but that's not the instrument in my hands, so I work with what I've got. He smiles and shifts up his hands a little, adding an off-beat count that would tie an orchestra up in knots in five seconds flat. Fortunately for him, I can count to five. I grin and remind myself to have a word with Quint. Our drummer is feeling feisty tonight, and it's maybe time he got a taste of what that can earn him with the right sub.

I spy our other two band members, both in a small group over near the front door talking to Ari. The crowd is thin yet, and we won't truly get rolling for a while, but something's going on over there. Scorpio looks pissed and a little embarrassed, Harlan is acting like he expects his sub to burst into flames any minute, and Quint's looking thoroughly amused.

I fiddle a little more with my melody line, but my eyes keep getting pulled back to the front door. Jackson simplifies his beat, so clearly he's noticed the drama in progress too. Sitting up on this stage is never boring, especially if part of your kink is liking to watch.

Ari blows a kiss at Scorpio and heads out into the foyer to greet someone. Jackson sounds a hand roll on his drum, which makes me laugh. I hope whoever's about to walk in the door is expecting to make an entrance.

Heads turn in the lounge. Kinky people read energy better than anyone, and all the oxygen in this room just got sucked toward the front door. Ari comes back through the swinging divider that separates the foyer from the lounge and turns to hold it open for the new arrival.

I see the sexy red dress first. Classy, vivid, and glued to the curves wearing it. And then I see her face.

I make it to my feet, but it's a close thing. I feel like a newborn colt trying to stand, and the wires and legs of my keyboard aren't helping at all. Especially since I can't take my eyes off the woman in red.

She's grown up a lot, but I would know those eyes anywhere.

Of all the sex clubs in all the world—Chloe Virdani just walked into mine.

Chapter Three

CHLOE

I expected many things tonight. He wasn't one of them. I can feel the surprise moving up my skin, setting every nerve ending on fire.

Ari slides a hand under my elbow and guides me forward, out of the doorway and toward the stage that holds a man I haven't seen in twenty-six years. I can feel my breath leaking out of me in stuttering, shaky spurts, and I try to pull myself together. It's a losing battle. Twenty-six years hasn't dimmed what he does to me at all.

"I take it you know each other," says Ari quietly.

That's far too weak a word. "We did, once. It's been a long time."

She doesn't say anything else. She just delivers me to the edge of the stage and melts backward into the crowd.

Eli hops down, a move that reminds me of the boy I once knew so well. He comes to a stop in front of me, his eyes the same soft, piercing gray they were at sixteen, and touches his fingers to my cheek. "Chloe?"

He asks it like it's a question, but we both know it isn't. My entire being sinks into his fingers. I reach up, taking his hand in mine. "Eli." I glance at the stage behind him, at the keyboard he just left. "You did it. You're still playing music." I'm careful with my words. We were once two army brats, and he was the one with the parents who didn't understand the calling inside him at all. Maybe this is just a gig he does once in a while. It doesn't feel that way, though. He feels like a man who knows what it is to live his dream.

The dream that once fluttered wildly in the chest of a boy and that I blew on with every bit of strength in my sixteen-year-old soul. Even when it meant I had to say goodbye.

He swallows, like he can remember that boy just as well as I can. "Yes. This is a side thing I do for fun. I'm first cello in the Seattle Symphony when I'm not here."

I can feel the tears rising. "You picked the cello?" He played four instruments well enough to be accepted to Juilliard, but the cello was my favorite, the one that spoke to the very depths of my teenage self.

He tips his forehead into mine. "Yes. I didn't bring it tonight. I didn't know you were coming."

I feel my laughter, shaky and jittery and real. "I didn't know until earlier today either."

He pulls me into his arms, and I can feel the boy—and the man he's become. The one who has all the boy's passion and none of his doubts. The arms around me are strong and certain and inviting something far less tentative than the Eli I once knew.

I exhale and lean into the hug. I feel his hand slide up my back, into my hair. Holding me against his chest. His breath teases the top of my head. "I really missed you, shorty."

I laugh. Even in spiky heels, he's still got more height on me than he once did. "That nickname is never going away, huh?"

I feel his chuckle rumbling against my ear. "Do you want it to?"

I don't. Growing up, moving from base to base every couple of years, I never had a history with people. I do now, but it's adult history. He knows parts of me I don't want to forget. "No. But I really don't think it's fair that you got taller." And a lot more built. I have my arms wrapped around one sexy musician.

"They fed me a lot at Juilliard." His voice is quiet.

I lean back in his arms, trying to reconcile the man with the boy who cried in my arms the night before he left. "You were supposed to go, Eli. I still believe that."

He nods. "I was. You were so much surer than I was back then."

I knew he needed to leave so the music that made him beautiful didn't have to die. "You got sure." I'd seen it in his letters. The ones we'd eventually agreed to stop writing.

They hurt too much.

And that isn't somewhere I want to go in a room full of people. I reach up and touch the scruff on his chin. The boy I remember would have killed for that much facial hair. "We'll talk."

He eyes me carefully, not letting go of his snug hold around my waist. "Are you staying a while?"

I nod, feeling short of words. "Yes."

The smile holds so much of the boy. "I'll come find you at my break."

His arms let go and I step back. I watch him walk onto the stage like he owns it—and like he doesn't need to be the star. Instead, a woman wearing torn jeans and a corset I designed steps up to the mike, electric guitar in her hands. She gives me a look that says she didn't miss a second of what just happened between me and her keyboard player, and then she strums a loud chord as she grins out at the audience.

I miss what she says next. I'm too distracted by the man rolling up his shirt sleeves in the background.

Chapter Four

ELI

I'm a professional musician, which means I know how to stick with the program even when half my brain is somewhere else. However, just because I have that skill doesn't mean I should use it. Not here. People here are observant, and a checked-out Dom is dangerous, even if all he's touching is a keyboard.

I shoot Jackson a wry look, because he just morphed his beat to something a three year old could follow, and get my head mostly back in the game. Scorpio's warming up the crowd, getting them going with some of our standard covers. Softening them up for marshmallow Quint and his ballad.

I'm trying to figure out which parts of me I need to firm back up.

I glance at the back couch where the siren from my past is sitting with Ari, looking for all the world like she's just stopped in for social hour. That's a skill she's always had, right from the first day of high school on the base in Heidelberg where we met. Me, I always looked like the new kid, even when I wasn't —awkward, shy, and a little lost unless I was on my way to the music room.

Chloe knew how to land somewhere and make it her own.

I shake my head as she elbows Ari and they both laugh. Apparently she still does.

Scorpio swings us into another one of our classics, which I suspect she's doing mostly out of kindness to me. I can't take my eyes off the girl who once dared me to make myself whole. I know why we lost touch, but in this moment, watching Chloe's sexy legs and laughing eyes and expressive hands, I want to kick my younger self around the block.

She meets my eyes and I see the same confusion that lives in mine. Two people trying to overlay this moment on ones that are a whole lot older. It's a strange feeling, like a chord progression that hasn't resolved. There's a tension in the air, a next step waiting to happen.

I add a flourish as Scorpio drags us into the chorus. Eli of the present, trying to reassert a little control—because control matters to me almost as much as the music. It's how I finally escaped awkward and shy and lost and became the person Chloe always thought I could be.

Right now, though, I'm more fascinated by who she's become. Her eyes are curious, wandering the lounge. Focused in particular on the subs in skimpy lingerie, which is interesting. I frown. She's not putting out a Domme vibe—just classy, self-assured poise. If I'm guessing, which is always dangerous from a distance, she's self-assured and vanilla. She's too obviously curious for someone who's spent any time in a kink club.

I realize where my head has gone and give it a mental swat. Trying to figure out if Chloe is kinky is putting the cart before a whole herd of horses. A lot can change in twenty-six years. She could be married, lesbian, or completely uninterested in the guy who once kissed her with far more ardor than skill. I know better than to read too much into trembling breaths and shaky legs at an unexpected meeting, especially when it was mostly me doing the shaking.

She might not know that, though. Doms learn some interesting things, and so do professional musicians, and pushing the nerves deep underground where they can't be seen has served me well in both of my chosen realms.

Quint comes up behind me and snorts. Loudly. I check— I'm still playing the same song he is, but it's fairly embarrassing that I have to check.

Chloe has visitors now. The boss man himself and the gorgeous ray of sunshine he convinced to be his sub and the love of his life. Chloe flows off the couch, radiating surprise and pleasure, and gives Emily a huge hug. Clearly they know each other—and clearly neither of them expected to meet here.

I aim a pointed look at the young, blonde troublemaker sticking to Chloe's right shoulder, who probably has all the answers.

Ari winks at me and turns to say something to Damon.

I growl. Quint snickers behind me and manages to mess up his guitar riff.

Scorpio turns our way, amused as fuck and looking like she might brain the entire band with her guitar. Which is a serious threat—they don't call us Doms on the Bottom for nothing.

She shakes her head at the two of us and steps up to the mike. "It appears we have some distractions that require our attention, so we'll be taking our break a little earlier than usual tonight." She raises her hand and waves at Chloe. "Hello, nice lady in red. Do me a favor and put my keyboard player out of his misery one way or the other. The songs after the break actually require his brain to be attached to his fingers."

The entire lounge is laughing, which was absolutely Scorpio's plan.

Chloe isn't. She's watching me. Waiting to see what I do next.

Chapter Five

CHLOE

I've been here less than an hour, and I already know I like these people—even when they're shining a spotlight straight into my soul.

Maybe especially then. I run a store that encourages people to let their underlayers be seen. There's a reason. I get the feeling that the members of this club would understand my exhibitionist tendencies better than most.

They're all watching as Eli makes his way over to me, but it's a supportive kind of staring. A room full of strangers, many of them half dressed, ready to catch us if we need catching. It feels like balm a teenage army brat didn't know she needed—and gives me my first real clue about why the man walking toward me has made his place here. Because clearly he has. He belongs, and not just up on stage. I'm good at reading people quickly, and Ari has been a fast, efficient tour guide. The man walking toward me is a Dom, even if I have a really hard time reconciling that with the boy I once knew.

He takes a seat beside me on the couch, crowding my space in a way that the last three people sitting there didn't. My breath gets wavery again, and I firm it up. There are things I need to know before I let him see me shake.

He angles himself on the couch and takes my hand. "So, of all the sex clubs you could have walked into, what made you pick mine?"

Sixteen-year-old Eli wasn't this bold. That used to be my turf. I'm not sure how I feel about that. "Ari invited me." I pause. He hasn't done anything to deserve the sudden snap in my spine. "I own an upscale lingerie boutique. We do a lot of custom designs, and she's hoping we might develop a line for the club."

His eyes light up. "You're Harlan's source?"

That's been the standard reaction all night. Instant celebrity status. "I am."

Eli shakes his head. "I have a card for your store. I've been meaning to drop by."

I don't want to ask why. Men don't usually buy lingerie for themselves. "Harlan has apparently been handing out a lot of cards." I'm glad Eli's is still in a pocket somewhere. Him walking in the door of my store would have been equally shocking, but it would have been different. I wear different skin on my turf, the less-vulnerable kind. It feels right that he sees me this way first.

He smiles and cups one of my hands in both of his. "So you came to check us out and see if you want to make pretty, kinky underthings?"

It's time to remind him I'm not sixteen. I give him the same level look I give Mandy when she forgets I'm competent. "I've already decided that much. This is a chance to observe my wares in their natural environment."

The light in his eyes is different this time. More dangerous. "For that, you'd need to pay a visit to the dungeon."

I laugh and pat his hand. I do still take dares, but I'm more selective now. "Have you forgotten how outrageous theater people can be? Nothing I see on the other side of that door is going to shock me." Even in high school we were pretty brazen, and my drama tribe happily let Eli hang around simply because he was mine. He might not have done much, but he watched plenty.

He doesn't seem like a man who watches from the sidelines anymore. He's recaptured both my hands, and there's a control there. One that dares me to try patting him again.

I'm tempted, but I've learned some things about starting fires since he saw me last. And I've learned to appreciate the first small flames, and not to blow on them too fast. "Ari is organizing a focus group for me, but tonight I'm just going to sit here and talk to a few people and keep my eyes open." I smile. "And listen to a band that's pretty fancy for a sex club."

His grin could melt every pair of panties I sell. "We like fancy here."

They like everything here. The fashion in this place runs from naked to grunge to high-end boudoir, which is going to delight my designers to no end. Eli's chosen look is elegant and understated. The suit he's wearing wouldn't look out of place in any of the best restaurants in town. I stroke the sleeve, appreciating the cut and the fabric. "You like fancy."

He shrugs. "I lived in Europe for a while and got used to dressing the role of dashing classical musician out on the town."

There are stories there, and I want to hear all of them. I like who he's become, and I want to know how he got there.

He lets go of my hands and runs his palms down my arms. "I'll be playing for a while longer, but I'd like to walk you home. Will you stay?"

He doesn't even know where my home is. That opens up

something tender and a little bit sore inside me. He knew everything about me once. "Sure."

He nods at the woman behind the bar, who is currently giving the band's other guitar player a kiss that looks like it's seconds away from going molten. "Meghan usually has something tasty she can serve up. Ask for something that isn't pink."

There's a story there, too—one that's amusing several people within earshot.

I'll ask Meghan. It will give me something to do while I wait for a walk that's either going to chase away the last vestiges of history wreaking havoc in my belly—or start forming them into something new.

Chapter Six

ELI

She waited. I didn't doubt that she would, but I didn't expect it to feel so good to see Chloe standing by the door, chatting casually with Ari and Sam and Harlan. She might not be part of my world, but she's clearly a welcome visitor. The three she's chatting with have been herding members her way all night.

Sam gives me a look as he leaves the group and meets me halfway. One that says I might have to go through him to get to Chloe.

I chuckle. Even at sixteen, she didn't need protectors. "Hey Sam—how's Soleil?"

He melts into daddy-shaped goo. "She made a sound yesterday that might be her first giggle."

I was there the day my niece did that. She held six adults hostage for several hours waiting for her to do it again. "Who managed to pry you off her long enough to send you to the club?"

The subs at the club have all learned their sulks from Sam. "Gabby. She said we can't be decent parents if we don't get out once in a while. Besides, I think Leo needed this. He keeps waking up at night, scared that she's stopped breathing."

I've seen their set-up—the baby sleeps in a cradle about six inches from Leo's nose. She will never lack for love, but she may eventually need to learn to fight for a little space. Or let Gabby do it for her. "I'll come by early to the barbeque on Friday and hold her while you make the tacos extra spicy." Sam's cooking skills don't range a lot wider than mine, but all of his options will set fire to your taste buds.

He shakes his head and pats my shoulder. "Sugar, you got beat to that chance by ten miles. Mattie's coming early, and she promised me extra-hot jalapeños from the market."

I clearly need to up my game, and in more than one direction. Chloe isn't looking my way, but Harlan's starting to give me dirty looks. It's time to figure out what to do with my siren in red before the big guy decides Chloe needs his protection. Unless she's changed a whole lot, she might punch him in the nose if he tries.

Sam grins and blows me a kiss. "Have a really interesting evening, Sir."

Sam generally uses that title right before he pulls one of his famous pranks, but I don't think that's his intention tonight. Probably because he knows I have my hands full already.

I make my way over to the small cluster of people at the door and step in to Chloe's side. "May I walk you home?"

She smiles at me, the light in her eyes not at all dimmed by the late hour. "If you don't mind a slow meander. I was trapped in my back room doing inventory all day, so I've got the urge to stargaze a little."

Harlan bristles behind me. "Nobody walks home from the club alone."

I ignore him. He's not wrong, but he should know better—he's got a sub who thinks she's invincible too. Chloe isn't going to take kindly to any man telling her what to do, especially if he's using Dom voice while he does it. I slide her hand into the crook of my arm instead. "Do you have a coat?"

She laughs. "No. I still run hot."

The sound Harlan makes this time sounds a lot more like laughter. I guide Chloe out the door with more haste than skill. I'm done with being a public spectacle. There's too much I want to know about the woman gliding into the dark beside me, and I don't need all of Fettered standing watch and offering commentary while I do it.

She nods us to the left when we hit the sidewalk, and breathes in the cool air of one of Seattle's spectacular late-summer nights. "Yes, this is absolutely what I needed, thank you."

Twenty-six years apart and apparently we've developed some new habits in common. "I liked to stroll around the cities in Europe where we played after our shows. I loved the shadows and the character and the lack of tourists."

"Shows?" She reaches out her fingers to brush leaves as we walk past them. "You weren't in an orchestra then?"

The pangs are gentler now than they were a few months ago. "I was part of a cello quartet. We toured extensively, mostly in Europe."

She's quiet for a moment, and I imagine she can feel the loss inside me. "What happened?"

"Nothing dire." Although sometimes, on dark nights, it doesn't feel that way. "The other three settled down to wives and babies and jobs that don't require them to travel the world. Sean's in Paris, Bojena's in Prague, and Leon is in New Orleans, at least for now."

"And you're here." Her fingers brush the inside of my arm.

I am—and somehow, that doesn't feel quite so random anymore. "The symphony wanted a cellist, so it was a chance to keep playing without the constant travel. I'm working on some material for a solo album. Once I'm ready to record, the others will fly in to play on some of the tracks." It was the best reason I could come up with to pull the three people who were the core of my existence for fourteen years back together.

"That sounds lovely and interesting and maybe a little sad, too."

She's nailed it—and started us into the conversation we need to have. I keep the pace slow. She asked to meander, and that fits the conversation I want to have. "Things change, but sometimes it's hard to know if they've changed in the right ways. If there was a different choice that might have worked better."

She chuckles. "They didn't get rid of your perfectionist tendencies at Juilliard, I see."

They honed them into an art form, but that's not what I want to talk about. "I'm sorry we lost touch."

She shrugs. "We agreed. It hurt so much to get your letters, and it felt like a piece of me wouldn't truly be mine again until I could let that go."

I lean over and kiss the top of her head. "Did it work?"

She smiles up at me. "I would have said yes this morning. Right now, I'm not so sure."

She's always been able to flatten me with her honesty. I tug us in the direction of the water. I don't know if I can find her stars tonight, but I can at least arrange some cool ocean breezes. "I'm not sure whether to ask about now, or about all the years in between. Who have you become, shorty?"

She snorts. "Someone that nobody would dare to call shorty."

I grin down at a scowl that would do a Domme proud. "I might need some kind of special dispensation."

She leans into my shoulder. "You might get it."

Chapter Seven

CHLOE

There's something rising between us, and it's so soft and tender I'm not sure what to do with it. He's always been able to find those parts of me, and I'm realizing just how few people in my life I let do that.

He heads us down a quiet residential street, one that's headed toward the water, but taking its own sweet time. "How long have you had your store here?"

That's an easier question than his last one. "Since a year after I graduated. I put myself through an accounting degree as a pole dancer. I knew I didn't want to be an accountant or a pole dancer, so I opened my shop."

His chuckle rolls out low and easy into the night. "Accounting?"

I grin. "Most people are more shocked by the pole dancing."

His fingers are warm in mine. "You always wanted to be seen. Do you still do theater?"

It was my life back when he knew me, and the reason I knew he needed his music. "In college, I discovered that making the costumes was even more fun than being onstage."

And the tribe was tighter, which filled my army-brat heart in the very best of ways. "Making theater costumes for a living is a good way to starve, so accounting was the backup plan I came up with one evening. There might have been martinis involved."

He laughs. "You went to college here?"

"Yes. Dad was stationed here for a bit. When they moved on, I stayed."

"Roots." He kisses the top of my head again. "You always wanted those too."

The gentle touches and kisses are calling me home, but I don't know if that's a place that exists between us anymore. "It sounds like you turned into a gypsy instead."

He shrugs. "I found my home in the music. In the four of us who played together."

He lets me hear the pain this time. "It must have been hard when that ended."

"It was."

Two words, spoken by a man resilient enough and strong enough to let himself hurt. I lean into him this time.

He runs a fingertip along the black lace peeking out from the neckline of my dress, sliding the dress aside enough to reveal a lacy strap. "Is this one of your designs?"

He's lighting up small fires under my skin again—and triggering my sense of self-preservation. "It is. You might find it easier to inspect in my shop."

He puts my dress back in place, but he takes his sweet time doing it. "You make beautiful things."

I take a big gulp of cool night air. "I wanted to make things that would last and feel wonderful to wear. Most lingerie stores sell terrible, scratchy garbage."

He meets my gaze carefully. "I know."

Chapter Eight

ELI

She doesn't duck her eyes. She wouldn't. Chloe has never run from uncomfortable. That used to be me. "Tell me who you've become, Eli."

I know what she's asking. It's time to have the conversation that began the moment she walked into my club. The one that is going to ask both of us to stand deep in uncomfortable.

She needs to know I can do that now. I get us moving again on our slow, inexorable meander to the water. "A fellow musician took me to a BDSM club in Budapest, a ritzy one where a foreigner in a nice suit was a hot commodity. I discovered that I liked playing with control and surrender."

She tilts her head curiously. "Both ends, or are you purely a Dom?"

Someone's been educating her. Probably Ari. "I'm a Dom. Music is where I find my surrender."

She smiles. "It's balance for you, then. There are parts of your life where you offer structure to others, and parts where you can let go and let something else do the holding."

She's just described kink beautifully. I raise a questioning eyebrow.

She grins, pleased that she's surprised me. "I make lingerie for a living. I think a lot about where to put structure and where to leave it out."

Damn. She thinks like a Domme. "You see that very well for someone who's never been in a kink club before tonight."

Her cheeks dimple. "You seem very sure about that."

I wince. Pole dancer. I'm forgetting crucial facts. "Sorry. Pretend that was a question."

She laughs and squeezes my arm. "The club where I danced was pretty upscale. It had a similar feel to Fettered's lounge, but the power dynamics weren't nearly as polite."

I blink. "That's not usually a word people use to describe kink." Especially on their first visit.

It's her turn to shrug. "The manager at the club where I worked did a good job of keeping the dancers safe, but I still saw plenty. I don't know the rules that govern what happens at Fettered, but they're lovely. When a woman wearing practically nothing can walk across a room and have several flirty conversations and never once get touched or leered at without her clear consent, that's a beautiful thing."

I don't know who she was watching, but any unattached sub would have gotten that kind of respect. "Not all clubs are that well run, but when it's done right, that's exactly how kink is supposed to work."

She glances at me, and I can see the color in her cheeks, even in the dim of night. "I was impressed. And a little daunted. It's going to be an interesting design challenge."

That's the first time she's tried to step us to safe ground. Which is like waving a red cape in front of a Dom. "How did it feel personally?"

She snorts. "You've gotten more direct."

Holding a paddle in your hand teaches that lesson fast. "There's a pretty intense vibe running between us. I want to know more about the shape of it. Part of that is whether you find my lifestyle interesting."

Her look is quiet and serious. "You're in it deep."

It isn't a question, but I answer anyhow. "Yes. It's as much a part of me as my music."

She's silent for nearly half a block. "Thank you for letting me know."

She's trying to head us to safety again, but I'm not done. "Remember how I used to play half a dozen instruments? For me, sex is like that. There are a lot of ways you can choose to be part of the music, but only some of them make my soul sing. The rest are fine, and fun for a Friday-night jam, and I do them well enough, but they're not where I want to live. Not where I *can* live and be whole."

She nods. "I've seen people like that give up theater. They bleed and it never really stops. I hope neither of us would let you do that."

She's never let me walk away from who I am. "This is the first time in a long time that I wish my insides were a little more flexible."

She smiles a little. "Maybe mine are. I don't think I'm kinky, but I've never really asked the question."

I thrive on power imbalances, but this one sucks. It asks everything of her and so little of me. Other than holding steady, even if what lives in my core might be the reason we both need to walk away.

She stops abruptly and turns us face to face. "Show me."

I stare down at the parted lips and laughing eyes of a woman who totally intends for me to kiss her.

She slides her hands up my flummoxed arms and grins at me. "I'm an actress, Eli. I understand through doing. I need a demonstration, please."

All the remaining notes fall off my sheet music. "What?"

"I watched tonight. I understand some of what you play with, but I don't understand how it feels. I'd like to, because I'm still too curious for my own good, and because it's important to you." She touches her fingers to my cheek, gently repeating her obvious invitation. "So kiss me like a Dom would."

I groan. If this two minutes is any indication, I'm about to kiss Fettered's next trainee Domme.

She leans into me and my Dom training finally gives me a good swift kick upside the head. I run my fingers into her hair and take a good hold, reveling in the way it flows over my hand. I tip her head back a little, holding her away from my lips. Unbalancing her. Sending her hands flying to my shoulders.

That will work. "Keep your hands there, shorty."

Her eyes widen in surprise, and she pulls against my hand in her hair, testing.

I keep holding the structure. Letting her feel it. Using my fingers in her hair to keep her head, her very kissable mouth, exactly where I want it. I close the gap and tease my tongue along her lips. Intentionally denying what she thinks she needs. Offering up something that might meet a deeper, bigger need.

Or not.

Chapter Nine

CHLOE

Who is this man and what did he do with my soft, sensitive, tentative Eli?

The hand in my hair tightens and angles my head a little more. His lips trail down the line of my jaw, the side of my neck. Not softly. Darting licks. Nibbles. Ones that almost hint of pain.

Every inch of skin on my body pebbles.

He chuckles, low and deep, and runs his free hand up my ribs and cups my breast. His fingers find my stiff, suddenly aching nipple and give it a squeeze.

Fork, meet light socket. Wiring I didn't know I had shoots sparks into places nowhere near my nipple. I stare at him, and I'm pretty sure my mouth is hanging open for reasons that have nothing to do with the kiss that hasn't happened yet.

He pulls me in tighter against his chest, and I'm suddenly aware of just how much he's holding me up. I squirm, needing my feet back underneath me.

"Stop." It's a sternness that has my eyes flying back to his. "Stay where I put you."

My legs feel like they're made of marshmallow goo. "I'm off balance. I don't want to fall."

"Hush." He punctuates his words with a light kiss this time. "You wanted to know how a kiss from a Dom feels. Be quiet and learn."

I want to tell him where he can take his orders, but he's right. I did ask. And this is Eli, who used to hold me for hours while I talked and cried and worked through all of my teenage spilled milk. I tell my objecting muscles to stand down, and consciously relax into his hold.

He smiles, and there's approval in his eyes. "Beautiful. Thank you."

My spine nearly stiffens again.

He leans in and nibbles on my chin. Works his way over to my earlobe, using the hold he has on my hair to guide my head. The movements are almost random, not related to where his mouth is traveling at all. Slowly, my neck stops trying to guess where he wants me to be and simply lets him put me there.

He tilts his head, and his soft curls brush the fingers I have resting on his shoulder. I lift my hand to touch his hair and he growls. "Keep your hands where I told you to keep them."

I'm not at all sure I like this bossy Eli. "I want to touch."

"You touch if I tell you that you can. Not before."

That doesn't sound like fun for either of us. "How do you get pleasure from that?"

He tips his forehead into mine. "Do you get pleasure from being the boss of your own store?"

On the days that don't involve inventory or crying brides. "Yes."

He brushes his knuckles against my cheek. "I get my pleasure, I just take it differently than how you imagine I should. Forget what you know, Chloe. Just let go and see how this feels."

I realize how hard I'm fighting against doing just that. Slowly, I unclench the knotted muscles in my back, the ones trying to snap my spine straight against all of this, and sink into where he's trying to put me. Let his hand support my head again. Notice how safe and held I feel—and how shaken, all at the same time.

"That's it." His lips are traveling my neck again, his breath finding all the hollows that make me quiver. His fingers roll my nipple, more firmly this time, and my new wiring runs a current straight to my clit.

I pull against the hand holding my hair. I need to do something. Resist. Melt. Hide my face.

He firms his grip and turns my head to nibble my ear, rubbing the scruff of his beard against my cheek. When he bites down hard on the lobe, my whine of protest morphs into something that sounds almost like begging. His mouth is on mine in an instant, hot and demanding and swallowing the long, liquid moan that runs up my throat.

My brain implodes. This isn't sixteen-year-old Eli. This is a man who knows exactly what he wants and how to take it.

Chapter Ten

ELI

The sounds she's making are shooting rockets of need straight to my cock.

Which I need to ignore, because the woman in my arms isn't at all clear she wants to be there. Not like this, anyhow. I was waiting for her brain to disengage and it finally has, but her body signals are a mess of confusion. Which is making all my Dom senses cringe. I don't know if I'm kissing a woman with a sub inside her or not, and asking for surrender if she doesn't want to give it goes against everything I believe in.

Except for the part where this is Chloe and kissing her again feels like coming home.

I gentle my mouth on hers, not sure whether I'm doing it because I'm a Dom who likes to play with rhythm or because I need to be home more than I need to be in control.

Her lips tremble against mine as she exhales. Her moans have quieted into a hum, one full of pleasure and bliss. I tug a little on her hair, listening to how it changes the notes.

Interest. Uncertainty. Curiosity. Resistance.

A song that hasn't found its melody line yet.

The one inside me is much clearer. The happy, lilting joy of my fingers in her hair. The rich low notes of my nose drinking in the smell of her that has never been anything as silly as strawberries or flower petals or spices and has always been purely Chloe.

Her hands squirm on my shoulders again.

Damn. This is supposed to be a demonstration. I nibble on her lower lip, giving it a sharper bite and running my tongue over the stinging hurt.

She growls, a sound full of pleasure and intent, and nips mine.

I growl back.

Her body freezes, but I don't have to use words this time. She remembers the experiment, the rules I laid out so very poorly. Her hands settle back on my shoulders, and her body molds back to mine.

Compliance. Willing enough, but not nearly complete.

I brush my lips over her temple. We're not going to get an answer tonight, and whether she might want to someday play sub to my Dom is only one of the questions we're out here asking. I'm so very tempted to walk her around the corner to my new condo with the sleek lines and sexy artwork and see if I can pick up where sixteen-year-old Eli was dumb enough to leave off. She's absolutely luscious, and I want her as badly as I want my next breath.

She's also written deep into my DNA, and that's why we're still standing out here on the sidewalk.

She sighs in my arms and rests her cheek against my shoulder.

I don't want to let her go, and she clearly doesn't want to leave, but this song doesn't have anything that resembles a melody yet, and my need to protect that is sudden and hot and fierce. We need time. I could take her to my bed, but I don't know what either of us need there yet. Underneath all her strength and self-assurance, Chloe might have the bones of a sub—or she might not.

I tuck my cheek against the top of her head and breathe in the intoxicating scent of the woman who just walked back into my life. "We need to talk before we take this a whole lot further."

Her laugh is breathy and pleased and frustrated and real. "That isn't what I was expecting you to say."

It isn't what I want to say, but some parts of me are a lot smarter than they were at sixteen. I tip up her chin so that I can see her eyes. "There's lot of fire here. I want to talk so that we don't burn things that matter."

Her need dissolves into tenderness. "There he is."

I don't need to ask who. I can hear him too.

The sixteen-year-old boy who never stopped loving her.

Chapter Eleven
ELI

I punch in the special access code for the band and let myself in Fettered's front door, cello under my arm. I'm hours early, but the acoustics in the lounge are surprisingly good and I need somewhere to play and think.

A plan that lasts just long enough to walk in and spy Quint behind the bar, drying glasses and doing whatever it is bartenders do when they have no customers.

He raises an eyebrow in my direction. "Hey. Scorpio call a practice session I don't know about?"

"No." I lean my cello against the bar and take the glass of sparkling water he pushes my way. "I'm supposed to be in symphony recording sessions for another three days, but apparently the woodwinds don't have the brains of worms, so they're in extra rehearsals and the rest of us got sprung."

Quint looks amused. "Worms?"

Our conductor isn't the most tactful guy in the world. "One of his lesser insults." Which we all tolerate because he's really good at his job, and because if any of his worms ever need anything, he's always the first guy in line to make sure it happens. I've only been here six months and even I know he's gold.

Quint switches out his drying towel for one to wipe down his already pristine bar. "How's the lady in the sexy red dress?"

Kinky people suck at small talk. I shrug. I don't have an easy answer for him.

He snorts. "How are you?"

Underneath the hard-ass, this guy is gold too. "I'm not sure. I feel like I'm halfway stuck in a time warp. Hard to get my head into the right place." Made harder by my trip down memory lane this morning. The shoe box didn't take long to find. I'm used to traveling light, but that, I've always kept.

"Harlan and Ari really like her."

That's a leading statement if I ever heard one. "I really like her too. And back when I was a gangly teenager, I loved her as deeply as I was capable of loving anyone."

"What happened?"

No judgment—but no dodging, either. Which is probably what I need even more than a couple of hours in a dark corner with my cello. "Our dads were stationed at the army base in Heidelberg for three years. It only took a week of that before we were inseparable. Then her dad got transferred to Hong Kong and I got a full-ride scholarship to Juilliard."

He winces. "That must have sucked."

Nobody back then understood just how much. "It did." My hand grips my water glass too tightly. "We're old enough that the Internet didn't exist yet. We wrote letters for a while, but she asked for them to stop, because she's always been the brave one. They hurt too much. I felt like a hole ripped open inside me every time I got one."

I huff out a breath and try to lighten things up a little. "We were kids. It was deep and intense, and then it was over."

Quint's wearing a look that says he's a softy, way down deep —and he doesn't believe me at all. "She was your first?"

The photos I held this morning put me right back inside that gangly teenager. "She was my first everything."

His lips curl up into a faint smile. "Then your life just got really interesting."

That's one way to put it. "We're not the people we were twenty-six years ago."

He nods quietly. "You got kinky. And she runs a lingerie store for vanilla people."

I don't say anything. Sometimes it's the pauses in the music that have the most power.

Quint wipes all the way down to the end of his bar and back. "She might be able to go there."

I don't need to ask him where. "Maybe. Her brain would be willing to try, I think. But I kissed her last night, and it didn't feel like kissing a sub."

Quint grunts. "A Domme, maybe? She's got the self-assurance."

I make a face. "That would suck for me."

He laughs. "You ever been the submissive?"

I shake my head. "No, you?"

He laughs again. "Hell, no. Do you know what kinds of evil torture devices they have for cocks?"

I do know. Enough to be very sure it's not my space. "If Chloe's a Domme, Ari will drag it out of her." Especially if the two of them are going to be hot and heavy on the lingerie project together. Ari's not good at leaving kinky stones unturned.

"You'll know first," says Quint quietly.

I reach for my cello. In the light of day, minus the stars and the romance and the hot allure of Chloe in my arms, I'm afraid I already know. But I promised us time last night, even if she didn't hear me say it, and I'm going to make sure we get it. Which means I need out of the fingers-on-chalkboard happening in my head. And since I apparently don't get to hermit with my cello, I need a distraction. "Want to work on your ballad?"

He shoots me a suspicious look.

I unwrap the red velvet that keeps my instrument warm at night. "I was thinking it could use a cello line under the guitar. Or maybe just the cello and you singing." If I'm right, it will be a really interesting addition to my solo album.

And a reminder that sometimes unlikely love actually works.

Chapter Twelve

CHLOE

I grin at Sam and Ari, who are sitting on the low rock wall that rings Fettered's yard and waving at me. Sam's dressed in something that only three people in Seattle would be brave enough to wear outside in daylight. I scan it with a professional eye as I approach. He might be a scantily clad harem boy, but whoever made his outfit does quality work.

I kiss his cheek, because it only took ten seconds last night to know he's one of my people. "Nice costume. Who made it?"

Ari laughs. "Hold that thought and let's go around back. Harlan and Emily are waiting, and they'll be mad if we don't share you."

She leads the way to a small side garden, set up with a beautiful wrought-iron table that looks like Emily's had her way with it. I smile at the wedding planner who has sent more referrals my way than I can count. She's currently sitting at the table sipping tea in a bright sundress, looking like the last person I'd expect to find at a sex club.

One of last night's happiest surprises. I smile and take the vacant chair beside Harlan. Emily pours me a cup of tea.

The big Dom scowls and picks up a cookie. "I don't know why I'm here."

I lean over and kiss his cheek too. "Because you're my best customer and I want to keep it that way."

He turns bright red, to the delight of everyone else at the table.

Sam snickers and winks at me. "I knew I liked you." He breaks a cookie and hands me half. "So what do you need to know to make us pretty, sexy things, sugar?"

I've done a lot of thinking about that. Insomnia is good for business planning. "I'd like to work on a list of basic design principles—elements that you think are essential to everything, and options you'd like to have. In particular, I'd like to know where vanilla lingerie is letting you down."

Harlan scowls. "It doesn't come off."

Emily pats his arm. "It does if you take it off before you tie your sub up, sweetie."

He growls at a tea cup that doesn't look at all scared of him. "I like her tied up."

A clear and obvious need, and one he's never said a word about in all his trips to my store. I relax. This is just like theater costumes. They know what they need—I just have to ask the right questions. I pull several simple pairs of lacy underwear out of my bag and lay them out on the table. "Let's say we're trying to modify something simple like this. Ties on the side? Hooks?"

Harlan's scowl vanishes, replaced with interest instead. "Ties can be dangerous. Dangly bits don't play nicely with impact toys."

Emily leans forward, fingering the lace. "Ties could be uncomfortable, too. What about a bra fastener, but on the sides?" She grins at Harlan. "Doms are good at undoing those one-handed."

He rolls his eyes, but doesn't disagree.

I jot down ideas on my tablet and pull out a lace-up corset and lay that on the table. "Sticking with the theme of a restrained sub for a minute, what would you want to be able to undo on this?" I put my wrists together. "I saw a couple of restraint positions last night, so I'm already thinking about how to make the straps detachable."

Sam picks up the corset, holds it up in front of his chest, and tosses it to Ari. "Not my size. Why don't you put it on and we can show her some of the positions we end up in?"

Ari promptly peels off her top and bra, talking as she goes. "It would be great if the straps could detach front or back. There are lots of restraint options where one or the other isn't easy to reach."

I'm managing to wrap my head around a serious business conversation with half-dressed people. Almost. Even theater people aren't quite this casual about their naked bits. "Can you show me a couple of tangible examples?"

Harlan reaches out, grabs Ari's wrists, and pulls her over his lap. Which, even corset half on, nicely demonstrates the strap-access issues they were just talking about.

Ari laughs and wiggles her ass in the air.

Emily's cheeks turn pink as she smiles at me. "That would be the one I'm usually in."

I've known Emily for over ten years, mostly in a casual professional sense. In one sentence, she's just invited me to join something deeper and a lot more fun. "Do you want me to make your underwear easier or harder to take off?"

She laughs. "I'm the sub. I don't get a vote."

I may not know her that well, but she has an impeccable reputation, and you don't get one of those in wedding circles in this town if you let anyone push you around. Which means she's choosing this.

"Mmm." Sam's hum is low and fascinated, and it's me he's looking at. "There's a question running around in that head of yours, sugar. Out with it."

There is, and the very self-confident people at this table would be the right ones to ask. "I'm not sure it's relevant to designing lingerie."

He just snorts and takes a sip of his neon-pink drink.

Ari grins. "It's pretty hard for a newbie to cross lines in this place just by asking questions." She runs her hands down the corset she's wearing. "And we want you to get really comfortable and stay, because this is the nicest thing I've ever worn and I want more of them."

I smile at her, because she's irresistible. "You can keep that one. I'll want all of you to test-drive samples for me, so if I could leave here with some measurements, that will keep my designers from beating on me."

Sam laughs and winks. "Maybe you should let them—you might like it."

I roll my eyes at him and try not to let my cheeks turn as pink as Emily's.

Harlan is watching me with eyes that have zero sexual intent but are peering into my soul anyhow. "You want to know why Emily's a sub. Why she's okay with not getting a vote."

I can feel my eyes popping.

Sam pats my arm. "The best Doms like us to think they're psychic, but really, Harlan's just good at watching and listening. And we were all there last night when you made Eli fumble his notes. You have history with a man who's a Dom now. Of course you're curious."

Harlan growls. "You're supposed to ask before you strip somebody naked, Sam."

I give the big Dom a stern look, the one I keep on reserve for mothers who step too far out of line. "I'm more than capable of handling a friend saying what we all know is true."

His eyebrows fly up.

Ari snickers. "I do like you, Chloe."

Sam cuddles into my side. "Are you going to save me from the big, bad Dom, sweetie?"

I can feel my abrupt stillness. I'm suddenly in a play with lines I don't know, and I'm not sure how I feel about that.

Emily shakes her head. "Stop messing with her, you guys." She looks at me, her eyes full of empathy. "It's hard to be new here. They're doing a terrible job of communicating, but they're doing what they do with all new people and giving you some easy, tangible ways to see if various aspects of kink appeal to you."

Someone is finally making sense. I flash her a grateful smile.

She smiles back. "You don't have an obvious submissive vibe, but some people don't."

I raise an eyebrow at Sam and Ari. They're the least obviously submissive people I can imagine.

Emily laughs. "Exactly."

I nod. "So I don't look like a submissive, but Harlan growled at me to see what would happen?"

"Growled at you and chastised Sam." Ari leans forward. "And you calmly told him to quit interfering. Which is what a Domme would do—a female top. Or a switch like me when we're choosing to play that role."

I'm a little annoyed at being a rat in a maze without them asking first, but I'm also fascinated. "What would a submissive have done?"

Harlan growls again and Ari's entire body language shifts. She orients to face him, eyes down, every line of her body expressing concern and compliance.

I can feel my body reacting. No. Just no.

Harlan growls again, this time at Emily. I can see her surprise. She doesn't change her posture like Ari did, but her entire attention focuses on the big man with the tats.

He smiles and touches her cheek. "Sorry, Em. Sometimes I forget how new you are."

Then he growls at Sam, and this time I can feel it, low and heavy, all the way down my spine.

Sam grins, scoots over, and plunks down in his lap, curling up like a sexy kitten. "I'm sorry, Sir. I think I need to be punished."

Harlan rolls his eyes. "Off my lap, Sam."

Sam cuddles in tighter. "But it's my warm, happy place, Sir."

"Off, or I'll tell Leo to lock up all your costumes for a decade."

I put the pieces together as Sam nonchalantly hops off and takes a seat back on his chair. I know theater when I see it. Other than Emily, who got surprised into being mostly herself, I just watched a very nice performance put on for my benefit. "You're telling me that submission doesn't look the same for everybody."

Ari beams at me. "Exactly."

"Eli already tried this with you." Harlan doesn't frame it as a question.

I nod. "I asked him to, but I don't think we got any answers."

He looks unconcerned. "Sometimes it takes a while to know. You might be a sub, or a Domme, or a switch like Ari here, or none of the above."

Not all of those possibilities fit with who Eli has become.

Emily leans forward, her eyes full of sympathy. "Give it

time. You're doing a really good thing by being curious. You don't need to rush it."

I wish I agreed with her, but I can hear the low, haunting notes of a cello flowing out the open window behind her. It's calling to me—and the music is already building its crescendo.

Chapter Thirteen

ELI

I look up from my fingerboard as I draw the bow through the last notes, somehow not surprised to see Chloe standing there. It feels like there are threads running through the ether, pulling us together.

Giving us a chance—or at least the haunting facsimile of one.

Quint's voice dies off along with the echoes of what I've tried to do to his ballad. He leans on his stool and looks Chloe up and down. Measuring. Doing his intake thing. Trying to figure out if the woman who's fallen back into my life might fit in my lifestyle.

Which I find surprisingly annoying.

Apparently, so does Chloe. She raises a wry eyebrow. "Your people outside already tried that. Nobody has any answers."

Quint shrugs and pushes off his stool. "You're not scared of me. That's one answer."

Chloe's other eyebrow goes up. "Is that a requirement? That submissives are scared?"

"No." My tone is shorter than I mean it to be.

Quint snorts and gives me the same scan he just gave

Chloe. "I like what you did to my song. I'm not doing it on your album. And now I'll be taking my not-scary ass to the office to deal with paperwork."

I make a face as he walks off. I was hoping he hadn't figured out the album angle yet.

"He wrote what you were playing?" Chloe takes a seat on the stool he just vacated. "It was lovely. Gravelly and captivating."

She's dressed simply today, in a sapphire-blue tank top and gray capris that hug her curves and make my hands want to cop a feel. It's probably a good thing they're currently full of very expensive instrument. "Thank you. It suits the cello really well. Now I just need to convince him to sing it in the recording studio."

She slides out of her sandals and somehow manages to pull her feet up and cross her legs. A very sexy, classy Buddha on a stool. "I was outside talking to some of the club members about the new lingerie line."

I saw Sam and Ari conspiring earlier. No way any conversation with those two was boring. "Was it productive?"

She grins. "Very educational."

I'm afraid to ask, but given the exchange with Quint, it feels like I need to. "They're all trying to figure out if you're kinky."

She nods. "They're your friends, and they'd like to see the puzzle pieces of your life fit together nicely."

That's probably a very kind way of describing what happened out there. "I don't need you to be a puzzle piece, shorty."

She chuckles, low and rich, and it warms places inside me that even music can't reach. "I know that. I have no intentions of being reshaped in ways I'm not happy with, no matter how appealing the offer."

I lean my cello against the wall in a casual move that would turn several faces in my orchestra white, and walk over to stand behind her stool. I run my fingers under her hair, lifting it from her neck, letting it waterfall over my hands. "There are more colors in your hair than there used to be."

She laughs. "I have a very nice man at a salon downtown who puts them there."

I steeple my fingers at the top of her head and draw them down her scalp, massaging slowly.

She moans quietly. "I remember the first time you did that."

I do too. We'd been doing our math homework and her head hurt. "I sat behind you on your bed and did this until your headache went away." It was the first time I'd truly touched her, other than the hesitant, semi-accidental contact of two teenagers not yet sure who they were for each other. "Then you curled up in my arms and slept until your mom called us for dinner."

Meatloaf and mashed potatoes. I ate three plates full, drunk on the feel of Chloe asleep in my arms.

She leans back, resting her head on my chest. "I have something I want to say to you."

"Good." I keep running my fingers through her hair. "I'm listening."

"It feels like there could be something between us. In the now, not just the echoes of history."

I kiss the top of her head. "Yes."

"I know that kink is a big part of who you are, and I have no idea if it has any part in my life. That's a pretty big, flammable unknown."

Even melted against me with my fingers massaging her scalp, I can feel how utterly solid she is. How much strength there is in her for us to lean on.

At sixteen, I just leaned. The Eli of now intends to appreciate her strength a whole lot more—and to offer a solid place for her to lean too. "Kink isn't everything."

In one quick, fluid move, she spins around to face me on her stool. "Exactly. I want to explore this, but I don't want that to be the fence I have to get over first. I'm willing to come to the club and to learn and to ask myself some questions and let other people ask them too. But while I do that, I want Chloe-and-Eli time."

That's what we called it. The quiet, tender ache in my belly remembers. Some of the sweetest hours of my life were Chloe-and-Eli time. "The grown-up version."

She's grinning at me. "Yes. With wine and nice clothes and interesting conversation."

I cup her face in my hands. "Can these dates include some hot vanilla petting?"

She laughs, and it washes over me, setting those deep places to vibrating again. "Yes. They can have some kinky petting too, but I don't want to feel like a lab rat."

I wince. "Sorry. You walked into a kink club and everyone pounced. Including me."

She leans in and kisses my lips. "I want you to pounce, sexy man. I just need you to do it in lands that I know."

I crouch down in front of the stool and kiss the fingers she has resting on her knees. "What about hot vanilla sex?"

She chuckles and runs her fingers through my hair. "We figured it out at sixteen. Let's see what happens."

That's exactly the kind of stumbling around blind in the dark that the kinky world tries to avoid, but if there are good reasons to say no to this woman, I can't find them. I groan and lay my forehead on her knee. "I can't believe I'm still saying this to you, but I have to go practice my cello now." So said the text message that arrived shortly before she did. Recording session in thirty minutes. Apparently the worms have learned.

Chloe laughs. Music practice was one of the few reasons we ever spent time apart.

I stroke her arms, loath to let go. "Can I take you to dinner tonight?"

She smiles down at me and nods. We have a date.

Chapter Fourteen

CHLOE

Eli opens the door to his condo as I exit the very swish elevator and step onto carpet deep enough to swallow my shoes. I walk the hallway, appreciating the touches of luxury in places they often get ignored.

He watches every step I take, his eyes a little hungry and a lot happy. It occurs to me just how easily I read him. Twenty-six years have changed a lot, but all of who Eli is still lives in his eyes. I hold out the bouquet of wildflowers I bought on a whim.

He chuckles and buries his nose in them, just like I hoped he would—I thoroughly annoyed the flower seller by sniffing all her wares. Then he holds them off to the side and buries his nose in me, running soft kisses up the sensitive skin of my neck. "Thank you for coming."

I smile and tilt my head to give him better access. "It's not a hardship. You live in a beautiful part of town."

He shrugs. "It's close to work and I like the view." He tugs me in so that I can see the panorama of trees and lake and far-off green hills through the sweep of windows that are clearly the reason this place was built. "And the soundproofing is really good, so my neighbors don't hate me."

They don't know what they're missing. Listening to Eli play would be high on my list of great features in a neighbor. I look around his space, trying to learn something of the man. It's not actually that large—there are thoughtful details everywhere, but this isn't the condo of someone who needs a lot of space to prove he matters. It's cozy, under the luxurious vibe. Comfortable seating and warm throws and colors that make it feel very much like an upscale den.

Eli leads me over to a loveseat in plush fabric that has my fingers stroking it as I sit down.

He chuckles. "That's what I did right before I bought it."

That doesn't surprise me. He's always explored the world through his fingertips. It took me a little longer to catch that bug—to understand the power of the right fabrics and textures to set a mood, or break one. "I like your space. It feels like a place I'd want to spend time."

He smiles, clearly pleased by the compliment. "I hope you do."

I can feel my cheeks get warm. I didn't mean it quite that literally.

His fingers slide under my chin. "That's an invitation with no strings, shorty. I don't know where we're headed, but if we discover the sexual chemistry isn't a fit or it fizzles on renewed acquaintance, I'd still be really happy to have you bring over one of your books and curl up in a chair and listen to me curse at my cello."

I laugh, because that memory feels like it's only days old instead of decades. "You still do that?"

"I do." He grins. "And after so much time touring in Europe, I can curse fairly fluently in a lot more languages."

I reach out and stroke his forearm, pleased he's wearing

something that gives me at least that much skin to access. If this chemistry is going to fizzle, it hasn't started yet.

He hums quietly, harmonic accompaniment to my fingers.

I could do this all night, except for the part where I'm starving. My belly is going to start singing along with his humming. "Maybe we should go eat before we do much more of this."

His eyes slide open. "I ordered in. There's a small balcony off my bedroom. I thought we could eat and talk with some privacy."

It's my turn to grin. "And a bed really close by?"

He laughs. "That depends on what we both want after dinner."

I came here pretty sure what I want, but I've learned to enjoy the process of getting there. Especially with a man who enjoys his sensual pleasures as much as this one. I stroke his arm one last time and stand. "Take me to your balcony, handsome."

He walks over to a bar counter that divides his kitchen from the rest of his living space and lifts up a bag. I laugh when I see the label. Thai food, from my very favorite hole-in-the-wall mom-and-pop place. "Lucky guess?"

"No." He slides his arm around my waist. "I called your shop and asked Mandy for your favorites."

That's sweet—and oddly bossy. "You could have asked me."

He's watching me carefully. "I could have."

I can feel my brain trying to decide if this is a lovely bit of caretaking or an end-run around something that matters. And my guilt that I'm suddenly bobbling this. "I'm sorry—I'm not sure why that's hitting me strangely."

He kisses my forehead. "Thank you for being honest. Can you tell me more about the strangeness?"

He really wants to know. He's studying me like nothing in the world matters more right now than whatever I'm feeling.

"I appreciate that you wanted to choose a dinner I would enjoy." I speak slowly, unpacking the feelings inside me. "I think maybe I'm still feeling a little sensitive to how control and submission are a big part of your life now. Part of me is wondering if that's what's going on here. A need to control." I shrug, my skin suddenly a size too small. "And I'm embarrassed to be feeling this way and causing wobbles between us and getting in the way of a really nice dinner."

Chapter Fifteen

ELI

She's still so unflinchingly brave.

I lean back against my bar counter and set down the food. I need both my arms for this. I reach for the woman who's working herself toward guilt for doing exactly the right thing. "Truth is the sexiest thing there is, Chloe. You're not wobbling anything. You're giving us a chance to show up for each other as adults. Thank you."

I can see her surprise. And I can see the edges of why takeout Thai has caused her to feel wobbly. I debate a moment, because we're supposed to be hanging out in vanilla territory tonight, but I don't know how to clean this up as a vanilla guy. "You're right. Me taking the time to learn your needs without asking you is absolutely a form of control. It wasn't intentional on my part, and I'm sorry for that."

She tilts her head, a little bemused. "Some of this stuff goes beyond the bedroom, does it?"

"It can. But this isn't about kink. It's about who I like to be in the world. I wanted to let you know that tonight matters to me, and that's how I chose to do it." I snug her in a little tighter to my body. "But it might not be the best way to communicate that to you, and that's what I want to understand."

Her eyes close, but not before I see the flickers of shame. "I'm sorry. I wasn't seeing it that way at all."

No wonder vanilla relationships crash into so many things. "That isn't your fault." I put enough firmness into my words that her eyes snap back open, and then I ask the question that matters. "I took control, and you felt it happen. Why is that uncomfortable for you?"

Her head jolts like my words landed physically. Her breath catches, and she pushes back against the clasp of my arms around her waist. Then she stops, looking down at her hands clenched on my biceps. "Huh. Apparently it still is."

I chuckle and soften my hold. "Keep following that thought."

Her hands start to move, up and down my biceps. Which makes it damn hard to concentrate. I focus on the wrinkles that form between her eyebrows as she thinks.

Her hands stop, and she looks up at me again, the bold back in her eyes. "Because when you take control, it takes something from me."

Almost there. "It gives you something too. If you want it."

She pushes out of my arms, but she's not running now, and I let her go. She walks slowly down the length of my bar counter. Brushes her fingers over the bag of Thai food, nodding slowly. Working it through. "Freedom. Space to be here and not worry about making my belly happy. A chance to feel pampered and cherished."

Thank fuck. I didn't completely screw up, other than entirely mangling the whole vanilla deal. "Yes."

She turns her head, looking off into the distance. Thinking again. "That part is really nice, actually." She takes a deep breath, blows it out, and meets my eyes. "But I think I need to give up the control, not have you take it."

That's not a line I hear often. "Tell me what you mean."

She pushes away from the counter, her feet taking her on a circle through my living room. A faster pace, matching her thoughts. "I have customers who special order things. Some of them have really precise requirements, and some of them want me to surprise them." She stops and looks at me from the far side of my coffee table. "But they ask me. I don't just surprise them if they didn't ask."

She's so very sure this is hard—that the words she's saying to me are some kind of terrible blow. I need her to understand they're a gift. "So this afternoon, when I invited you to dinner, if I had requested a chance to spoil and surprise you, would that have made the moment when I told you I'd called Mandy feel different?"

Surprise lands in her body before it hits her eyes. "Yes, actually."

She's so beautiful right now. I close the distance between us, flanking my coffee table and putting my hands on her hips. "Then you would have been able to see it as being taken care of and cherished."

She's nodding, but there's still puzzlement. "I'm not sure why it makes such a difference, but when you said it just like that, I could feel the tangle inside me relax."

I take her hand in mine and kiss her fingers. "That's because you need to give your consent before you give up control."

Her eyes widen.

I grin and kiss her nose. "Sorry. I promise to be as vanilla as possible for the rest of the night."

She's already shaking her head. "No, I hear that this wasn't intentional. It was my reaction that pushed us here, but you have some way of understanding what just happened that I don't. I'm still a little confused, but I like where it's taking us."

I kiss her nose again and pick up the food, because her stomach is growling, even if she hasn't noticed. "Food. I'll explain why consent matters so much in my world over green mango salad."

Her eyes soften. "You really did quiz Mandy."

I did, and now it's landing the way I meant. And I've learned something really important about the woman Chloe has become.

Chapter Sixteen

CHLOE

I push the pad Thai takeout box back across the table to Eli. "Me and my chopsticks, we're done." And still amused that we ignored the plates and very nice table settings he set out and ate straight from the boxes.

He grins down at the three noodles I've left him. "Some things haven't changed."

I've never eaten the last bites of anything. My signature act of two-year-old defiance, and I never gave it up. "I'm full." And so is my brain. Eli's explanation of consent somehow made it totally fine that I got my panties in a twist over him doing a really nice thing. I can feel his wise words percolating in me, even now. Control in his world is never taken. It's given. It may look like it's being taken in the moment, but that's just theater. Half my body weight in pad Thai and coconut chicken curry and green mango salad later, that still has its hooks in me.

What kink looks like and what it is are really different.

He leans back in his chair, setting his chopsticks down.

I can feel the air change. I'm ready. We've talked about everything else. Now that I'm not distracted by lemon-grass fumes and the sensual joy of watching Eli eat, we need to fill in some of the bigger, more intimate holes of our past. I stretch out my hands and lace my fingers with his. I know about the kink clubs in Europe. Time to learn the rest. "Tell me why you still walk alone."

His lips quirk. "That's where you want to start, is it?"

I've never been someone who's tiptoed around things. "Yes."

He nods and takes a slow, deep breath. "I spent fifteen years on tour with the same three people. They became my family. Romantic relationships were limited and generally died after a few weeks of exposure to my life. A friend introduced me to kink, and that became my way of getting my sexual needs met. I had a small list of clubs I visited. Europe isn't that big, so we were usually near one of them."

I let my brain process that. My sixteen-year-old self can admit that it hurts. And that I'm glad he has people who love him. "So, what, you had a girl in every port?"

He grins at my sailor reference. Our army dads frowned on those, so we tended to use them often. "Something like that. No long-term intimate relationships, but I didn't feel like I was missing out."

He didn't. He made the family he needed.

He leans forward and takes my hands. "You?"

Nothing as sexy as a sub in every major European city. "I had two relationships that lasted. The first was back when I was getting my shop started, and he wanted kids and a farm on the coast where he could make cheese."

Eli chuckles. "You were dating a dairy farmer?"

A very sweet one. "He is now. He's married with two sets of twins and all the cows he ever wanted." His wife sends me cheese every Christmas—she's very grateful I gave him up.

"It's hard to imagine you in that picture."

I shrug. It took a long time to make peace with the fact that I hadn't wanted to try. "I don't think we were the right people for each other. Not for the long term." But it had still hurt terribly to put the lost look in his eyes when I ended it.

Eli sighs, soft and sympathetic. "Sometimes it's hard to let go, even when it's the right choice."

That sounds like a man who came closer to a long-term relationship than he admits. "It was. The second one was easier. I met him when he was a junior lawyer, working hard and playing hard just like I was. As he moved up, he changed. He wanted someone on his arm, available at his beck and call."

Eli winces. "Just so you know, some Doms are like that too."

I raise an eyebrow. "Are you one of them?"

He takes another one of his deep, slow breaths. "In bed, absolutely. In life, no."

I tilt my head, watching his face. "Why the difference?"

His thumbs are stroking the delicate skin of my inner wrists. "It's like my cello—I need to put it down sometimes to be able to appreciate picking it back up."

"I'm nobody's accessory, ever." I smile at him. "But being your cello might be fun."

He groans, and his hold on my hands tightens. "Vanilla date, woman. You asked and I promised."

It's an odd sensation to have a man holding me to my own needs. Especially when I'm not sure what they are in this moment.

He lets go of my hands and refills our wine glasses. He's only consumed about an inch of his. "So, you left the really nice farmer and the jerk who wanted arm candy. Where does that leave you now?"

No place that felt at all unfulfilled until a day ago. "I have some sex buddies. And really great friends." Which, come to think of it, maybe isn't all that different from his traveling cello family and a woman in every port.

Chapter Seventeen

ELI

She's opened a door. We both have. Somehow, we've connected back together at a time when both of us are free to pursue whatever this is and wherever it's headed. There are no deep relationship wounds, no partners waiting in the wings, no jobs demanding more of us than a lover might reasonably be expected to tolerate.

And she wants tonight to stay vanilla.

I thought hard about what that means before I invited her into my space. The difference between vanilla and kink isn't in the hardware. It's in my willingness to push my partner out of her comfort zone. So for tonight, we'll stay in Chloe's. If I happen to use my Dom radar to explore some of the edges of where that is, that seems like an acceptable use of the skills I learned in my various ports.

A history she hasn't either rejected or swarmed to, and both please me.

I stand up and make my way around the table, never letting go of her fingers. It's time to have fewer inanimate objects between us. She lets me pull her up easily, and I can see the heat flare in her eyes. She knows where I'd like to take this.

I wrap my arms around her, enjoying the feel of warm skin and curves. My bed might be less than ten feet away through the balcony door, but I don't need to get there quickly. And I don't plan to head there without consent. There are some pieces of who I am that I'm just not willing to set aside. "I'd like to take you inside now, Chloe. I want to undress you and lie you down on my bed and take my sweet time getting to know your body again."

Her skin pebbles at my words. She arches into me, her hands sliding up around my neck. Her eyes are clear and bold as she runs her fingers through my hair. "As long as I get some time to do the same, I'm really good with that."

I tell my inner Dom to stand down. He's not in charge tonight. "Sure." I pull open the balcony slider door. "In fact, you can go first if you want." I might have better self-control that way. Or not.

She turns us so that I'm facing backwards, puts her hands on my chest, and glides us neatly into the bedroom. The flush rising up her cheeks is beautiful, and almost manages to make me forget that I'm coming perilously close to handing her the reins. She stops when my legs run into the bed, higher than most for reasons she likely isn't thinking about too hard.

I am. I'd like nothing better right now than to bend her over the edge, hands held tight behind her back, and see just how she responds to me holding her still and fingering her until she comes.

She leans in, slides her hands up to my shoulders, and grins. "Race you to naked."

I stare as she suddenly turns into the sixteen-year-old girl I remember, pulling her dress up over her head and giggling madly as she reenacts a moment that is forever seared into my brain. And then I stare some more, because under the dress are some of the sexiest scraps of red underwear I've ever seen, adorning a body that isn't remotely sixteen anymore.

She catches me looking and pauses in the act of dropping her dress in a pile on my floor. "You're not naked, Eli." Her voice is husky, and taut with need.

Someone doesn't want to do this slowly.

Normally that would be my cue to make sure she doesn't get to come for at least the next hour, but that's not the Eli I'm supposed to be tonight. I reach out and brush my fingers along the strap of her bra, down to the lace covering plush curves. "I'm kind of distracted at the moment."

Her fingers cover mine. Not stopping them, just seeking connection. Giving me a chance to make the next move.

I step into her, pulling her tight against me, cupping one luscious breast in my palm. "My hands are busy. I don't suppose I could convince you to unbutton my shirt?"

She slides one hand up to the top button. "Maybe."

I roll her nipple between my thumb and finger and notice her sharp intake of breath. "I can be more convincing."

She chuckles and undoes one button. "Both breasts would probably do it."

I tweak the nipple I'm holding a little harder. "I'm busy with this one."

She tugs me down for a kiss. "Bossy man."

She has no idea. I let go of her waist and slide my other hand up, cupping two lace-clad breasts. I knead them, using my thumbs to friction the lace over her nipples.

She tilts her head back and moans softly, skin pebbling with need.

I lean in to kiss the smooth, soft skin around her collarbone, up the side of her neck. She's delicious, and an enchanting mix of curves I remember and those I definitely don't.

She rests her forehead on my shoulder and undoes buttons all the way down to my navel.

I wait, which seems every kind of wrong.

Her fingers slide onto the warm skin of my chest, parting the shirt. She feels her way over muscles that Ryan insisted we all grow on his chin-up bar at the back of the tour bus. I've kept them, even though I don't ride the bus anymore. A strange kind of homage to a part of my life I still miss fiercely. I breathe in as she traces her fingers through the dusting of hair on my chest. I didn't have that at sixteen.

I have two nipples in my hands, taut with need and nicely warmed up. It's a true sadness to let them go. I pull away slowly, using the lace to make sure her skin doesn't forget me.

Chloe gasps and whimpers, all at the same time.

I manage to hide my grin. I know a few tricks sixteen-year-old Eli never dreamed of.

Chapter Eighteen

CHLOE

He's killing me and I haven't even made it out of my underwear yet.

My fingers have a hold on his chest hair that can't possibly be comfortable, but I can't seem to let go—it might be all that's keeping me vertical. A problem Eli solves by dipping down, scooping me up, and tossing me onto the bed. I feel it give underneath me. Deep, sinking luxury with no bounce.

This isn't a bed to be escaped easily.

I look up at him standing over me, still mostly dressed, with a loopy grin on his face. I'm not the only one remembering how this once was between us. The playfulness. The goofy spontaneous combustion of two kids heading hell-bent into totally new frontiers. I'm not the only one appreciating the differences between now and then, either. He's filled out into muscles and hard planes, ones strong enough to hold his fierceness and protect his softness.

Once upon a time, I was madly in love with both.

I reach for him, needing more connection than the gaze of his eyes. Appreciation I can get elsewhere, although I'm glad he likes what he sees.

He sits down beside me on the bed, slowly undoing the buttons of his cuffs. Never taking his eyes off me.

I tug on the sleeve, wanting the shirt off.

Something flashes in his eyes, and then it's gone. He grins at me and lets the fabric slide off his shoulders, dropping it onto the pile that started with my dress.

I eye his belt buckle, wanting that to go next.

He chuckles and lies down on the bed beside me. "You're in charge of buttons tonight, shorty."

A buckle isn't a button, but I have no plans to argue with him. I swing myself up to sitting, which brushes my sensitized nipples against the lace of my bra. I hiss in a breath and move to undo the clasp in the back.

His hand stops me. "That's mine to do." His lips brush over the lace, blowing warm heat over skin that's already tormented.

His other hand slides lower, to the lace between my legs. I moan as he finds the fire building there, rubbing soft lace against my most sensitive parts. I try to squirm away—I'm not done with foreplay yet. I have an entirely delicious man to explore, and so far, all I've managed to feel up is his chest hair. I push against his arm, which doesn't move an inch. "I want to touch you, Eli."

He lies back and sets a hand under his head. A one-man buffet, laying himself out for my pleasure. Except for the hand still between my legs, his fingers sliding under the lace and into parts of me desperate for his touch.

I grit my teeth and reach for his belt buckle.

His fingers slide deeper, rubbing firmly over my clit as they delve into my wet heat.

I manage to get the buckle undone, but it's a close thing. I stare at the button of his pants, not at all sure I remember what to do with one. I lean down and catch one of his nipples in my teeth, just as he does something sharp and wicked to my clit. I bite down harder than I intended. "Take off your pants. Please."

His chuckle is low and dark. "Since you asked so nicely." A sinuous jungle-cat move and he's back lying down on the bed, naked and bold and entirely unselfconscious.

My eyes want a chance to look, to just drink him in and get to know the Eli of now, but my hands don't have anywhere near that kind of patience. Or any other part of me.

I go to shuck my underwear and his hand stops me again.

Bossy man. I raise an eyebrow. "This is your idea of vanilla sex?"

His eyes soften. "Let me. Please. You're a present done up in some really pretty ribbons, and I want to unwrap you."

I stop, fingers under the lace of my panties, all of who I am melting at his words. Those are the feelings of the boy I once knew, but he never would have been able to say them. Only his cello knew how to speak about what lay deep inside a quiet, gangly teenager, yearning to break free.

This Eli has learned to use his words.

Chapter Nineteen

ELI

I can feel her, tilting on the edges of surrender—and I don't chase it. Don't give her the small push that would get her there. Because I promised, and I've already pushed her far enough with words that weren't intended to do anything but let me stroke my new playthings a little longer.

A request that's about to be entirely blown away anyhow. I can feel the volcano that has always been Chloe already starting to vent into my hands. At sixteen, it was a miracle to find someone else who lived with that kind of explosive passion inside them—and even more magical to find a way to share it.

The magic hasn't dimmed, and the woman who is offering it to me now is trusting me to catch what she's throwing. I pull her down to the bed beside me. Some symphonies start with a slow movement. This one is clearly headed entirely in the other direction.

There will be time later for slow.

I leave her lacy underthings in place—I like to look at them, and I have two fingers buried deep inside her that don't have any intentions of leaving. I move in, nuzzling her neck, feeling her curves meld into mine, and curl my fingers into her g-spot.

She jolts, and then her hands are in my hair, her mouth hot on mine, her body undulating in needy, demanding waves.

One day I want to tie those waves down and send them down a narrow channel of my choosing, but not today. I curl my fingers again, giving her something to ride, and focus on the mouth under mine, catching the whipping end of the electric current I'm setting off in her pussy and sending it right back down again.

She writhes, arching up against me with hot, incoherent moans.

Her teeth close on my earlobe. "I need you inside me. Please, Eli."

I remember the first time she said those words to me. And the last. I pause a moment, head on her shoulder, suddenly staggered that I have the honor of hearing them again.

She turns her head so that her cheek lies against mine. Breathing together. Remembering. Two older, wiser people, drenching ourselves in the wonder of a second chance.

This isn't going to be vanilla sex—it's going to be the soul-melding kind. I keep our hearts joined and move my hips just enough to position myself at her entrance. I slide into fierce, wet, welcoming heat. She jolts again as I bury myself inside her, and her legs wrap around my back, seeking purchase. Pulling me deeper.

I pull her knees up onto my shoulders and lever myself to a better angle. I slide in again, slowly, touching every part of the inferno, making sure she can handle hard and fast this way. Her eyes meet mine, full of fire and need. I can feel lace frictioning my cock, because I somehow forgot to unwrap her before I buried myself inside her.

It doesn't matter. I'm here now and I'm not going

anywhere until what's barreling toward us smashes us both into willing stardust. I sink my cock deeper in short, quick thrusts, watching each of them land in her eyes. Her heels push on my shoulders, finding the leverage to join us even tighter.

I stay deep and rock, giving her what she needs to go over.

She wiggles away from the pressure an inch or two and slams her hips back into mine, insisting that I come with her. And then we're two frenzied, moving bodies, racing toward the volcano's mouth as hard as we can run.

It's a storm over as quickly as it began, leaving two sopping wet, boneless, shuddering people in its wake, with bits and pieces strewn all over the beach and no idea how to gather them all back up again. I hold her close, listening to the rasp of our combined breathing, feeling her heart pounding in rhythm with mine.

I don't need to calm us anymore. Don't need to hide the volcanoes back underground.

It's the gift that control has given me.

I hear her breath get more ragged—and then I feel the splash of wetness on my shoulder. The part of my heart that has always been hers staggers. I reach my fingers to touch the tears slowly running down the cheek that isn't buried into my chest. "You still do this." The first time she cried after we made love, it flattened me. Terrified me. It took a long time to understand that's just the last splutters of her volcano.

She cuddles into my side, soft and pliant and still vibrating, her voice husky with her tears. "Apparently so."

I kiss her forehead. Witnessing. Giving her the Eli that is no longer scared of tears.

She raises her head her eyes soft and wet and lucid. "I haven't, though. Not for twenty-six years."

Chapter Twenty

CHLOE

I smile down into sheets that smell like the morning after a really great night—with a side of bacon. Apparently someone is making breakfast.

Since I don't put it past Eli to put bacon and eggs into a stir fry, I find the muscles that attach to my arms and push my face up off the mattress. An act that's rewarded by an amazing view of Seattle on a sunny morning.

I imagine Eli picked this condo for the view—and the lack of view the neighbors have through his windows. I feel like a bird waking up in a really cushy nest, one with indoor plumbing and something wondrous underway in the kitchen. I sniff again. I would get up just for bacon, but I'm pretty sure there are coffee undertones. And singing.

My heart does the melty thing it's been doing randomly through the night, every time Eli woke me up and several times he didn't. I've always been a light sleeper, especially when the dial is turned up high on my emotional state. Even gooey with sleep and craving bacon, I can feel the potency of what happened last night sluicing through me.

It wasn't the really great sex, although that was entirely,

wildly memorable. It was the certainty, somewhere deep inside me, that my soul knows this man in a way that lasts forever. That my life would be rich and beautiful walking beside him. Which is a crazy amount of meaning to throw on less than twenty-four hours, but whatever rose inside me to meet him last night doesn't give a damn.

I sigh and push the rest of the way to sitting, curling up with my chin on my knees. The feelings rising inside me are so very primal—and so very innocent. They don't even know what kink is. They don't know how hard I resist being controlled, even when the intentions are entirely well meaning.

This is the pure yearning of the place inside me that cried when I left my farmer and stayed with my lawyer, the wild and free waif at my core who just wants to be seen and loved. I've never known quite how to tell her that there's more to me than a dancing child, but I've always known she's the very best part of who I am.

She wants Eli, and I can't blame her. The rest of me wants him too.

I shake my head and blink away the tears. The sun is out, I just had a night of spectacular sex, and a really hot guy is making me breakfast. I need to live in that and not in what-could-be. I slide off the bed just as he opens the bedroom door and walks in bearing a steaming cup of coffee.

He grins. "Please tell me you eat breakfast naked too."

I laugh. His good humor is contagious, and there is so much desire in his gaze. "I own three stores' worth of sexy lingerie. I'm rarely naked."

He hands me the coffee, lips quirking. "I like taking sexy things off."

Or torturing me while they're still on. I breathe in deeply, letting the aroma of coffee and happiness wake up the sleepy parts of my soul. "I smell bacon."

He sits on the bed, bends down, and runs his tongue in a quick circle around my nipple.

That's just going to get him coffee on his head and burnt bacon, although the instant heat between my legs would be very happy to get onboard with his plan. The waif, however, needs me to go somewhere else.

I tip my chin down, resting it on the top of his head. "We need to talk, love. Before I get sucked in again by your very talented tongue."

He gives one last lick to my nipple and looks up, awareness in his eyes alongside the happiness.

I want so very much to find a way forward that lets us hold on to both.

He stands up, takes my coffee, and holds out his hand. "Come. I've got bacon and eggs ready and toast that might be a little too crispy."

His calmness somehow reassures me. I noticed it last night too. This Eli doesn't waver when the going gets tricky—and he values naked honesty maybe even more than I do. I breathe out and take his hand. We're both stronger than we once were, and wiser. If there's a way, I trust that we'll find it.

And if there isn't, I trust that we'll find our way through that too.

Chapter Twenty-One

ELI

I can feel it warring inside her—the hope and the fear. Even the lure of bacon and eggs hasn't silenced it altogether.

I wait until she finishes a second helping. I know what we need to talk about. Last night hasn't changed the need for this morning's conversation, it's just increased its importance. The shape of the rest of my life is on the line. Which might sound melodramatic to anyone who isn't sitting at this table, but I can tell she feels it too.

"I'm not going to leave, Eli."

I look up to find her watching me. She smiles. "I want to say that much first. Some of last night was about sex, but some of it was about us being two people who have always loved each other right down to our toes. That part stays. No matter what."

I slide her fork out of her fingers and take her hands, exhaling fear I didn't even know I was holding. "Deal."

She smiles, and then her eyes get a little sad. She curls her legs up into sexy Buddha pose and sighs. "I know why I like to have control in my life. Tell me about why you like it in yours."

I know what she's asking. Whatever it might say on her business card, she's been a theater major her whole life. And I remember how she used to prepare for her parts. It was always about motivation—understanding her own and that of the other major players on the stage.

She wants to know why I'm a Dom.

It won't be enough for me to *tell* her, but it needs to start there. I tug on her hands. I want this conversation happening without a table between us. I guide us over to a long leather chaise and sit down, copying her Buddha pose. She takes a seat facing me, her knees touching mine.

Just like when we were sixteen. Which gives this conversation a place to start. "We saw a lot of control growing up." The army is full of it, and being a really unimportant side cog in very big machinery isn't all that much fun. Especially if you're not particularly cog-shaped.

She nods.

"A lot of that control was just part of the culture. It didn't feel like it had a purpose, or even when it did, it often still wasn't very nice to the people being controlled."

She's listening carefully, her whole body parsing my words.

"I ran from that for a long time. I controlled me and I controlled my music because I'm a better person when I have some structure to live in. But I tried really hard never to do that to anyone else."

Her smile is soft and warm. "I remember."

She always gave me so much credit.

"Then one day I walked into a kink club and discovered that for some people, control is a path to freedom."

She made a face. "That's a hard one for me."

I give her a wry look. "For me too. It kind of broke my head for a while." I pause, and then I head straight for what might be rough waters. "But you know a person like that. Harlan told me about Mandy, who works in your store."

Chloe stares—and then she starts to laugh. "Oh, man."

I love how smart and agile and freaking honest her brain is. "You give her a structure to work in, yes? And she thrives."

She nods. "Yes. It's not about sex, but I take your point. I do it for brides all the time too. Some need me to be the riverbanks to help shape their self-confidence, or to hold the noise at bay long enough that they can figure out what they need."

Her words are beautiful—and they slice at my insides. She gets, all too well, why it is that I do this. "Yes. In the kinky world, a Dom provides those riverbanks."

Her chin tips down. Really, truly grappling with my words.

When she looks back up, her eyes are clear. "That history, the culture we grew up in, it shaped me too. Maybe it made me into someone who instinctively knows what Mandy needs, or a fussy bride. But I'm also the person who got cranky with you last night for ordering me dinner."

Vanilla Eli doesn't know how to banish her guilt over that, but he needs to try. "Being really sensitive about control isn't a bad thing, shorty. It's just something to know about yourself so that you can have those needs met."

Her face scrunches up into something cute and confused.

I lean forward and kiss her nose. "Your vanilla eyes see what happened last night as something you want to avoid doing again. My kinky ones see it as something I'm glad we talked about so that we can use it in future to feed the connection between us. You're sensitive about control. That's not a landmine, it's an opportunity."

I can see that I've surprised her—and I love the wary, interested look in her eyes.

I also know that I want to leave it there for a while. I'm a musician and a Dom. Timing is everything. I lean forward and kiss her nose again. "A walk, more bacon, or vanilla after-breakfast sex?"

Her giggles spurt out all the way from her belly.

I'm really glad she doesn't choose the bacon.

Chapter Twenty-Two

CHLOE

I want to strangle them all.

I allow myself one blissful moment to admit that in the vault of my own head and then I pick three silky camisoles off the rack, in the size the maid of honor should have been trying on in the first place, and head back to the dressing room.

Nothing makes me quite so crazy as women who don't want to own their own shape, especially when my shop is full of quality, beautiful pieces specifically designed to give every kind of body a chance to shine. The rose cami will look absolutely delightful on Deirdre if I can get her to try it on. And if I can pull the blinders off her eyes long enough for her to really look.

There's nothing I like better than the astonished look in a woman's eyes when she looks in the mirror and discovers that she's beautiful. And sometimes nothing more frustrating than getting there.

All of which is keeping my conversation with Eli this morning hammering a beat in the back of my head. I've spent the last two days thinking there can't be a good reason, a tolerable reason, an attractive reason to want to be a Dom. And the last two decades using control as one of my primary life tools —and if I'm honest with myself, I know that I use it mostly for good.

Which means this can't be about judging Eli's choices any longer. I have to think about mine. If there are good reasons to take control, perhaps there are good reasons to surrender it too.

Mandy lifts the camis out of my hands. "I'll take these back to the change rooms. You take care of him."

I don't have to turn around to know who she means. We only have one customer who puts that look of panic in my assistant's eyes. I don't bother to hide my amusement as I turn around and smile at the big man wearing a black tank top that shows off his gorgeous ink. "Scaring my staff again, Harlan?"

He chuckles and comes to stand beside me. "You think she'd be used to me by now."

Mandy gives what she needs to receive—lots of care and feeding and very few field trips outside her comfort zone. However, I don't say such things out loud, especially to excellent customers with impeccable observational skills of their own. "What brings you by my shop today?"

He grins and fingers the nearest piece of lace. "Scorpio's birthday is in a couple of weeks. I might have bought everything in here that would suit her, though."

He's not wrong, but now that I've met the feisty woman who puts that look in his eyes, it's not hard to venture beyond what hangs on my racks. "That's enough time for a custom order, if you're interested."

The relief on his face would be funny if it weren't so sincere. "That would be great." He pauses and looks a little sheepish. "Do you have any ideas?"

I shake my head and take hold of his arm. "A dozen of them. Instead of lingerie, what about something for her to wear while she sings? Something sexy in leather, maybe with some decorative chains?"

His eyes light up. "She might even wear that without me spanking her first."

I hear Mandy's gasp before I see her trembling hands, reaching for the panties right behind us that match the rose cami.

Harlan winces, looking thoroughly apologetic.

Not his fault. Mandy skulks behind racks better than anyone I know. It comes with the territory of being short and matching the merchandise. I smile and hand Mandy a stack of rose-colored panties. "She'll want the medium ones, but try to get her to take the large. She'll hate us less if the wedding pictures don't have panty lines."

My assistant nods, easily distracted by a customer in need. And by her oversized desire to avoid thinking about a world where people get spanked and like it.

Harlan watches Mandy walk off. "Sorry about that. I didn't see her behind you, but I should know better than to bring that kind of talk in here."

For some reason, that makes me angry. "You're welcome in here as exactly who you are, with whatever conversation you want to bring."

He raises an eyebrow.

I sigh. "Sorry. I know I've created a brand here and Mandy fits it down to the ground, but some days I don't. I like it when you come in. You remind me that the world is a big, interesting place. I don't want you to dim down to match the merchandise."

He smiles. "You do something important in here. You make women feel special, help them feel proud about how they look. That makes the world a bigger, more interesting place."

All this from a guy who will go home and order Scorpio over his knees and turn her ass red. Or at least that's her story. Probably his too—I've never actually asked.

Harlan is watching me, his head tilted. "You've got a question. Ask it."

I do. "Why are you a Dom?"

He waits a long beat before he speaks again. "Are you asking the right guy?"

I know all about using pauses for effect. "Am I only allowed to ask one?"

He chuckles. "That's not up to me."

I'm not going there.

He leans back against one of my racks, which miraculously doesn't roll and dump him on his ass. "Because I'm more like you than I am like Mandy."

I stare, not at all sure how my assistant keeps ending up in these conversations.

Harlan grins. "You work differently with customers than she does, right? She cajoles them. You stuff them down a funnel and make sure they come out the other end."

I've never thought of it quite that way, but he's not wrong. "Her way takes longer. I don't have the patience."

He shakes his head. "Bullshit. It's not about time. You'd take as long as it needed to do it your way. It's about control and arrogance."

I can feel my eyebrows crawling up my forehead.

He laughs and wraps an arm around my shoulders. "Mandy gives a customer what they want. You give them what they need. Which is arrogance on your part, but also responsibility."

I squint, working it through. "Responsibility to get it right."

He nods. "And to watch and listen and pay attention so that you do."

His words are making crystal-clear sense, even if I wish they didn't. And they're driving home Eli's point. "I'm good at that. I always have been."

Harlan runs his hand down a mountain of panties, setting the lace to fluttering. "Yup. You might make a good Domme."

I grimace.

He squeezes my shoulders. "Or you might be a sub who can really appreciate someone holding that kind of space for her. One who knows that being brave and heading into the uncomfortable unknown rewards both of you."

My breath is stuck somewhere right under my throat. His words feel like jewels that I need to collect and hold and treasure—even if I eventually decide to throw them away.

I lean into his side, taking the comfort he's been offering since he got here. And the steel. Riverbanks, if I want them.

Chapter Twenty-Three

ELI

Sometimes the band hits a practice session and everything gels, four people melding into one purpose. Those days are gold. This isn't on track to be one of them.

Scorpio tosses her guitar down on a couch and heads for the pitcher of water on the bar. She glances at me, and I know she's not checking in to see if I want something to drink. Of the four of us, Scorpio and I have the most experience with small-group music and all the ways it can crash and burn. She's looking for a judgment call. Some days it's better to just take a break and try again when everyone's loaded up on carbs, sex, and sleep.

Or that's what always worked for four cellists, anyhow.

I stand up from the keyboard and head toward a couch that's reasonably free of instrument clutter. Break time. I'm not in the mood to bang my head against any more musical walls. I don't think I was the problem on the last song, but I wasn't fixing it, either.

Jackson stays behind his drums, socks on the ends of his sticks, practicing a rhythm that would tie most professional drummers in knots. He's loaded with talent, and I suspect he's even better on the hand drums he mostly plays outside these walls. I nod his way. "How's the yoga studio gig going?" Some smart person hired him to play for a class or two. Last I heard, they were on their knees begging for as much of his time as they could get.

He grins and keeps his hands moving. "It's good. I'm having to turn down hours now, and it leaves my nights free."

Yoga people go to bed early. Which leaves Jackson time to explore this new side of his life. I think he'll make a good Dom. He watches and he doesn't miss things. He's also doing very little besides watching, but that's not my problem. Quint kicks his ass out onto the floor periodically, and some of the groupies are getting smart enough to throw some looks his way.

"So." Scorpio puts a glass of ice water in my hand and takes the other end of my couch. "What's up with the lady in red?"

I raise an eyebrow at Quint. "We're sure Scorpio is a sub?"

He grins. It's a question that gets asked at least once a practice. "Harlan says so."

Scorpio ignores us. In this foursome, she's the top and she knows it. "Ari says you know her from way back."

Ari talks too much, although she wasn't the only one quizzing Chloe two nights ago. "Our dads were stationed over in Europe together when we were teenagers. We were two lonely army brats." Which doesn't even begin to do what lived between us justice. I take a long swallow of cold water. "She was my first love."

Scorpio's eyes soften. "That's really sweet."

Quint snorts and drops into a chair near the couch. "Whatever. How does she feel about being your sub?"

Scorpio winces and tosses a cheese doodle at his head. "I was trying to be subtle, asshole."

Both of them are about as subtle as rocket launchers.

"She's not kinky, or at least it's not anything she's ever explored."

Quint shrugs. "That's true of a lot of people before they walk through our doors."

True enough, but I don't think it applies here. Chloe walked in on business. "Even when we were teenagers, she totally owned who she was. If she was a sub, she'd know it by now."

Scorpio snorts. "Some of us are slow learners, even when we look like we have it together."

I smile at her. "You already knew kink, sweetheart. You just called it music."

She chokes on a cheese doodle and curls over, coughing. "What?"

Quint chuckles and swats her between the shoulder blades. "Music is all about surrender. Good practice for a sub."

He's got half of it. "Good balance for a Dom, too."

The look on his face says that part isn't a surprise to him either. Smart man. Hard-ass he might be, but he's a really smart, insightful one.

I helpfully swat Scorpio between the shoulder blades again. Can't lose our lead singer to a cheese doodle. "Being a musician is all about surrender. Leading music requires latex pants."

She eyes me skeptically. "I'm not a switch."

Which is a good thing, because marshmallow heart or not, Harlan is a Dom down to his bones. "Most of us who like to play with power are switches in some sense. We have parts of our lives where we want control, and parts where we want to let go." Which is a much more eloquent summary of the clunky conversation I tried to have with Chloe this morning.

"Huh." Scorpio stares at me, considering. "So if that's true, then maybe the amazingly together Chloe wants a place where she can let go too."

So I'm hoping. I let my friends see the terror and the hope.

Scorpio reaches for another cheese doodle. "Ari's ready to recruit her into the club of ladies in latex pants."

Much as it pains me, I want Ari to try. A long time ago, Chloe wanted me to be everything I could be. It's part of the reason I'm a Dom now, and I work hard to pay that forward. I just don't think Chloe needs my particular brand of helping people become who they're meant to be. "Maybe that's where she belongs. But honestly, I think she's vanilla."

I have really good evidence that vanilla sex is still Chloe's jam.

"Maybe." Quint guzzles water from a beer mug. "Someone that confident and sure of herself who's hardwired for kink, yeah, she'd know. But some people have flexible wiring." He gives me a long look. "They need a reason to be kinky."

He's straying into dangerous territory. I know it can work —I've got a really good friend with a baby on the way because it did for him. But Leah blossomed as a sub. I don't know that kink has anything to offer the woman I held in my arms last night.

The woman I want to hold again.

Quint and Scorpio exchange a glance that's full of things I don't want to hear. Thankfully, Jackson is just listening avidly. He's a baby Dom, this world almost as new to him as it is to Chloe. Except he knew he wanted to be here, knew something inside him belonged in this tribe of people who play with power and control and surrender.

All that's pulling Chloe through this door is me.

Chapter Twenty-Four

CHLOE

Ari's busy at the front desk with a group of people who are wearing less than the average lingerie model, so I shoot her a wave and skirt around them. I have an open invitation to sit in the lounge and chat, and that gets me past her with a wave and a grin.

I don't want to sit in the lounge tonight, but she's not the person I'm here to lean on about that. We have a different relationship, a professional one, and I don't want to get those wires crossed. I suspect we could both handle it, but my gut is leading me elsewhere and I've never ignored it. Not even when it gives me answers I hate.

I head straight for the bar, smiling at people I know and keeping my feet moving. Tonight isn't about work.

Quint sees me coming long before I get there, and whatever he reads in my body language has him waiting with a glass of sparkling water, a bowl of chocolate nibbles, and a neutral face he probably thinks I can't read. I slide onto a bar stool and take the water and a handful of chocolate. "I bet you win at poker all the time."

His lips quirk. "I bet you don't."

He'd win that bet. Theater people suck at poker. We're too used to wearing emotions on our sleeves, even if the emotions aren't our own. "I'd like a tour of the dungeon."

That makes him blink, which I suspect is about as much as I'm going to get out of his body language without his explicit intent. He pours a second glass of water and comes around the bar, taking a seat on the stool next to me. "Does Eli know you're here?"

That's got all the cards on the table fast. Which I think I wanted—there's too much at stake here for me to play a subtle game. I've always been better at direct, anyhow. "He knows I'm coming to the club some evenings for work. He doesn't know I'm asking for a tour."

Quint raises an eyebrow. "Does he know you want one?"

Tricky question. "I don't know." I take a sip of my water. "I hear that a good Dom can read minds."

He snorts. "A good Dom knows how to create the right mystique for subs who need that. You're not one of them. Smoke and mirrors will never earn your trust."

Harlan wasn't wrong about the arrogance. And Quint is mostly right, but it amuses me to poke at where he isn't. "Theater is magic if it's got the right person behind it."

Quint nods silently. Point to me.

I'm pretty sure I'm jousting with the wrong Dom. "Will you give me a tour?"

He raises an eyebrow. "Why me?"

Because he's the biggest hard-ass in the room and I trust him to tell me if I'm making a mistake. "Because you know Eli and you like him."

A snort. "He makes me play way too much classical shit."

I recognize a feint when I see one. "I wasn't aware he *made* you play anything."

A long silence. "It must be really strange to have known someone inside and out once and be trying to catch up."

I close my eyes. He heard what I wasn't even aware I was saying. All the points to the hard-ass on the stool, looking at me with empathy I can feel through my closed eyelids. "Strange, and wonderful, and important." I can feel it calling to me. A partnership of hearts with a man I have always loved.

I need to know if I'm going to break either of us before I say yes. "Whatever there is between us isn't going to go slowly. I need to know what I would be walking into, and for me, the best way of doing that is to try it on." I look over at the door to the dungeon. "I know how to do a walk-through of a part. I need to see what's in there, Quint. All the talk in the world isn't going to answer this for me."

He huffs out a breath. "Normally I'd tell you that doing the walk involves trying some things."

There's only one person I could try them with. I'm here trying to avoid that. "I pushed him away once because it was best for who we needed to be. I'm not sure I could do it again." I'm not shiny and bright and sixteen anymore. I know it's not so easy to find someone who can see every speck of your insides and love you anyhow.

Quint sets down his glass. "I have some choices here."

Interesting that he's not giving them to me—although, in a way, maybe he is. "And those are?"

"I could call Eli."

I've learned enough of the theater of this world to know that's what he'd probably do in most cases. "Or?"

He looks amused. "Or I could tell you that you don't get to walk through the doors of my dungeon without him."

I've done my homework. I know he trains most of the new members. His word is as good as a barred door. "Or?"

His amusement vanishes, and his poker face along with it. He looks down at his drink, but I don't miss the naked vulnerability in his eyes. "I'm going to tell you this as a Dom who's freaking gone and fallen in love." He looks over at me, and his intensity catches my breath. "Don't do this without him. Let him be there for you."

I open my mouth to protest, but his eyes stop me.

"I know you're strong enough to do this alone. You're also strong enough to decide whatever you need to decide with him standing beside you. You don't need to do this behind his back."

That hurts. "I was trying to do it on my own two feet."

"I know—but he won't see it that way."

Damn. It's the Thai food all over again. Perception matters. I can feel my resistance evaporating. "All right, I'll call him."

Quint's fingers wrap around my closed fist. "You protected him back then, didn't you?"

I can feel the tears rising. Twenty-six years of not being sure I did the right thing. "Yes."

Another squeeze of my hand. "It's time to stop."

Chapter Twenty-Five

ELI

Ari raises an eyebrow as I walk into her domain. "I thought you were staying home tonight."

Apparently news hasn't traveled. "Chloe's here. She wants a tour of the dungeon."

Ari's fast at the math of our lifestyle. She'll know how long ago my siren in a red dress passed by her gate. I keep walking. Ari isn't the woman I'm here for. I make it halfway across the lounge before I spot her, which has more to do with my nerves than the quiet corner Chloe's tucked away in, chatting with a couple of subs.

I catch Quint's attention. His text arrived shortly after Chloe's voicemail and got my ass out of recording edits and into Dom gear. He nods back at me, and I'm not sure what to make of the look in his eyes.

It doesn't matter. This is my scene coming up, not his. Because whatever Chloe might think this is, she's just asked for a Dom at her back, and I'm fucking glad she decided to let it be me.

The two subs sitting with her take one look at my face and

melt into the woodwork. She looks up at me, amused. "I didn't realize scaring people was your kink."

I take a seat beside her and kiss her cheek. "It's every Dom's kink, shorty."

She makes a face, but we both know the nickname's going to stick. "Thanks for coming."

There's only one way to have this conversation, especially with a woman who's never inched anywhere in her life. "How were you planning on doing this before you called me?"

Her shrug is wry. "I thought Quint might give me a basic walk around and let me gather some information."

He would have done it for most people who asked. I'm grateful he didn't this time—and curious about what he saw that stopped him. "Why did you want to do it alone?"

Her eyes soften. "Because I can feel what there could be between us, and it's not going to go slowly."

I'm not sixteen anymore. "If we go."

There's pain in her softness. "Yes. I wanted to know more before I got you involved." She sighs. "Maybe I walk in there and take one look and know it's not for me."

She wouldn't be the first, but I came here to be her Dom. "If we walk in there, I want you to give it an hour."

Her eyebrows go up.

Welcome to my world, shorty. "The club has safewords. Yellow if you need to hit the pause button, red if you need to stop. You can use those."

Realization dawns on her face. "You're treating this like a scene."

I don't know any other way to walk a woman around a dungeon and keep her safe. "Yes. My job is to see that you get what you need in there. Your job is to trust me to give it to you."

Pain leeches out from her eyes over the rest of her face. "Even if it means I can't be what you need?"

That's a conversation for after the tour. One where I maybe introduce her to some of Quint's shades of gray and flexible wiring. I lean my forehead into hers. Letting us both take strength from the answer that I know is the right one for now. "Even if. You've always been honest with me, even when it's really hard. Whatever you learn in there, we'll deal."

She takes a moment—and then I feel her leaning. Putting weight on the emotional wall I just wrapped around us. Giving me what I crave as a Dom.

Trust.

I run a knuckle down her cheek. "Give me a minute. I need to check in with one of the dungeon monitors, see what's going on in there tonight." There are some things she needs to see, and more than enough members hanging out in the lounge to provide them on short notice.

Chloe nods at me, a little uncertain.

I let her stay there. One of the first and most important things I learned as a Dom was that growth, clarity, and pleasure all arrive more strongly when a sub starts the journey on wobbly ground. I hold her eyes a moment longer, promising her that steady exists, just not on her own two feet, and then I head for Harlan.

I need a woman in latex pants, stat.

Chapter Twenty-Six

CHLOE

Three Doms have messed with me in less than a dozen hours. Harlan and Quint left me grateful. Eli's left me shaking and we haven't even started yet.

He feels different in this skin. More solid. Less likely to sway in the wind, and yet I've seen him lose himself to the music right here in this room. He still knows how to sway.

I laugh quietly to myself. He's like a good corset—he's learned how to add some structure.

Two hands land on my knees, and there's a face, eyes crinkled, smiling up at me. "What's got you amused, shorty?"

I'm not sure he wants to hear about the finer points of corset making—and this feels like the end of a ball of string. One I need to keep following for a bit to really understand what it is. "Something I'll share with you later."

He raises a surprisingly stern eyebrow. "I'm going to hold you to that."

He's putting his Dom skin back on. It's fascinating to watch. It's like some of the very best actors. They don't layer on a fake persona—they let themselves change shape. It teases at me. I want to know more of this new shape of Eli, even as it scares me. Even as I'm afraid it asks something of me that I don't want to be.

Which is precisely why I'm here. To feel out the shapeshifting of this world. To see if any of it feels like it could be me. I hold out my hands.

He clamps his fingers around my wrists and pulls us both up to standing. "Two rules. One, you tell me about all the ways you feel. No holding back to protect me."

I know he hasn't been talking to Quint, but I'm feeling a little too naked right now. "It's to protect me too, Eli. You're going to have to give me a little time and space to figure out how I feel in there."

His face morphs into something sharper. Firmer. "Time you'll get. Space you won't. Not unless I hear you say red."

His words do something strange to my belly. I'm not sure I like it, but I'm definitely affected. "I don't know if I can do this under pressure." I wince at my own words. Can't has never been a word in my vocabulary. "Scratch that. I don't know if I *want* to."

He laughs. "There's my shorty."

I have a strong urge to kick him in the knees.

He runs his hands up and down my forearms. "There are two kinds of dungeon tours, love. One kind is where you're a tourist gathering information. The other kind is where you let yourself breathe in what's in there and feel the power dynamics up close and personal."

I sigh as realization hits. "That's why I asked Quint for a tour. And why he said no."

Eli growls. "He said no because he knew I'd turn his favorite guitar into splinters if he waltzed you in there."

I start to laugh—and then I realize he's dead serious.

The jiggle in my belly is back.

I take a breath to try to settle it, but there's no time. Eli somehow has me moving, headed toward the door to the dungeon with a hand on my back, almost like he's trying to keep me from finding my balance.

I catch Harlan's eye as we walk through the door—and hear his words echo in my head. *A good Dom doesn't give you what you want. They give you what you need.* Tonight, Eli wants to be the one shaping the riverbanks. I feel my head tipping down, accepting what he's offering, before my mind knows I've made a decision.

I feel him stand straighter beside me. Wrapping himself around me with his energy, his breath, his absolutely focused presence. "Thank you."

I don't ask him how he knows. Eli has always known.

I tip my head back up and look around. My first impression is one of backstage during dress rehearsal, an almost overwhelming blanket of sound, raw and hard on my ears and very much like the bowels of the theater. The actors are different, though. Their stage isn't out through the curtains. It's here and now, and at least half the people in this space are currently audience, not entertainment.

My heart beats faster. I close my eyes. This isn't a world that wants me to make sense of it. Everything in here is an invitation to immerse—or to run.

Eli bends to my ear. "We're going to take a slow walk. My choice of where we go and how long we stay."

I can feel my spine stiffening in protest—and the audible smack as it runs straight into the steel of whatever he's wrapped around us. The steel that demands my trust. That insists I let go of meeting my own needs and hand it over to him. My breath catches in my throat. This was supposed to be a tour, but it has so very clearly become something else. Somehow, I've taken the step I was trying to avoid.

The one where I step into his world.

I'm not scared to be here. I'm scared of where I might need to step after I'm done.

He tucks his fingers under my chin and presses upward, infinitely gentle, as he turns my face to meet his eyes. "This is how I know how to hold you best in here, Chloe. If that's not what you want, use your safeword and you can leave or have Quint do your tour."

He wants to be the one who does this for me, I know that. But I don't see that need in his eyes at all. All I see is me. This wonderful, brave man, putting himself aside and letting this be all about me.

Riverbanks. I've seen them serve so very many people.

Time to see if anything in me wants to be water.

Chapter Twenty-Seven

ELI

I see her consent before she turns back to face the music of the dungeon, eyes closed and chin dropping down. Listening. There's no fear in her—just spit and fire and curiosity and the wild generosity that's always flowed from the deepest part of her.

My job tonight is to let her stretch to the healthy edge of that and no further. Even if it means letting her walk away.

I take a fast, experienced read of the lounge. Harlan gave me a quick download on the action and not much has changed. There are half a dozen major scenes in progress and some minor ones—new pairs feeling each other out or more experienced players showing greener ones some of the ropes. Literally, in some cases—it looks like Matteo is doing a demo of his Japanese bondage skills.

That might be an interesting one to watch, but it will be a while before he has his sub trussed up.

I can see Ari helping Tamelia, one of the club's veteran Dommes, set up a hasty scene along the back wall. Tamelia casts a quick look at the woman at my side, scanning her body language. Most would read Chloe's current posture as classic newbie sub, but I can see that Tamelia doesn't. Which nicely supports my instincts—and makes my heart hurt.

I steer Chloe toward the back corner. Tamelia isn't ready for us yet, and I'm not ready for her. Tank and Eva have a basic bondage and spanking scene going on in the corner, and Eva's hamming it up enough to have drawn in a sizable audience. Tank isn't sure enough of his skills yet to have put them on display in the middle of the room, so his exhibitionist sub is pulling the audience to her. Which her Dom is rapidly figuring out, given the wry look on his face as we walk over.

I don't spend much time watching the two of them, though. I'm far more interested in the reaction of the woman tucked in to my side. Her eyes aren't on the floor anymore. Chloe's scanning the action, taking in the watchers and the hulking guy wearing a gray shirt that doesn't hide a single one of his muscles. She looks at Eva last, right as Tank's hand lands on his sub's ass and she howls like he just split her in two.

I catch Chloe in mid-takeoff to launch herself between them. "Get past your first impressions, shorty. Really look."

Tank swings at Eva's ass again, and she howls—much to the amusement of the audience, because he stops his hand just before it connects. He growls, and she has the wisdom to look abashed. "Do that again and I'll give you something to scream about."

Chloe winces beside me. I hold my breath, willing her to see beyond the army-sergeant language to the layers beneath. To Eva's need for drama and noise that doesn't cause any damage. To Tank's growing certainty that his big hands haven't actually done a woman he deeply cares about any harm. To the high-voltage trust running between them like a living thing. All dressed up in the language of a big guy about to beat the crap out of a tiny woman while she's tied down and utterly defenseless.

Tank swings again, connecting this time. Eva squeals, with slightly more decorum, and Chloe winces.

I breathe, waiting. Sometimes a sub needs some help seeing the beauty under the violence. Sometimes she can't see it at all. And sometimes, in moments I've always been proud to be a part of, she can find the way herself. I keep Chloe tucked in tight to my side, saying with my body what I haven't yet said with my words.

Two more heartbeats and then I hear it. The soft whoosh of breath as something catches Chloe's attention. My ears tune in to the quiet music of her dawning curiosity. To the slow shifting of her weight off the balls of her feet. To her shoulders, letting go of her ears, and breathing that no longer moves in time to the beat of Tank's hand.

She's not just seeing the layers. She's been caught by one.

I try to follow my sub's line of sight, because I can't actually tell what has her intrigued. Ari catches my eye from behind Tank and wraps her fingers around her own wrist.

Bondage.

I take note of Tank's really basic tie-downs and lean over to my sub. "Tell me what you see."

"He's hurting her."

"She wants him to."

A long, shaky breath. "I think she does."

I can hear two things in that breath. She's definitely seeing some of the layers—and she has no desire at all to trade her ass for Eva's.

I ignore the sad shrinking of the hope in my heart. Impact play is a common kink, especially in a dungeon, but it's not the only one. We'll keep walking. Keep watching. And I'll give her another look or two at hard surfaces meeting bare asses. Sometimes first impressions are wrong.

Chapter Twenty-Eight

CHLOE

We're leaving Tank and Eva, and I'm grateful. I've met them both, and my head knows that Eva is at least as capable of saying no as I am and Tank would be absolutely horrified if he did anything to abuse her trust, but the rest of me is having trouble getting past the fact that this is what the two of them want to do together.

Past that fact that this doesn't feel like anything I ever want Eli and I to do together.

I don't know enough about what he likes. I could probably still take a good guess at his favorite foods and his favorite music and the things he dreams about at night, but I don't have a clue what his kinks are. I just know he has some, and right now that feels like a deep, dark chasm.

He doesn't say a word. He guides me over to another spot-light, shining down on a table where the action is a lot quieter —and far more intense. A woman I don't know is thoroughly strapped down. There are wide leather straps over her legs in three places, her arms, her belly, her forehead, cupping her breasts. She's spread-eagled enough to be on display, but that's not what anyone is watching.

A couple of feet above her belly, a candle is tipping.

The man holding the candle smiles slightly and lets a single drip fall on her quivering skin, just below her belly button. I can see the trail he's been making from the valley between her breasts. I can see where he's going.

The woman barely reacts as the next drop lands, but the small shiver that shakes her makes more noise than all of Eva's yelling. I hear how loudly I'm breathing and quiet it. There aren't as many people watching here, and all of them are caught in the hush of hot wax meeting skin.

Eli's hand brushes down my back.

Every hair on my body orients toward him, but I don't take my eyes off the woman on the table or off the man who is utterly focused on the trail of waxy tears he's building. Her eyes are closed and his are glued to the candle wax, but they're as attuned to each other as any two people I have ever seen. Melded together by small splatters of falling molten wax.

His control is absolute—and it's all for her. For what builds between them.

He lets a drop fall on his inner wrist and lifts the hand holding the candle a little higher. The next drop heads straight for the valley between her legs.

The sound that comes from her is a glacier cracking off into the sea, an iceberg chipped off her soul by hot wax and the man holding it. Her muscles tense, pushing against the straps. Telling me what I already know. They're not melded anymore. She's fighting this.

Eli straightens beside me, the hand on my back a wordless warning.

I know better than to speak. The hush of this moment is fragile and taut and filled with impending doom—and somehow holy. The eyes of the man holding the candle have gone from focused to utterly, unmistakably tender. Those of a man watching his love do a hard thing, the very hardest of things, while six people watch and breathe together and somehow try to will her back into the place of melting.

I already know it won't be us who gets her there. It will be her, and her trust in the straps and the candle and the man who's offered them for her journey.

Another drop.

Another cracking. This one causes her Dom's eyes to cloud with pain, but his hands on the candle remain absolutely steady. A man looking hard in the eye and not flinching—so that maybe the woman on the table can too.

Yet another drop, and this time her reaction is less sharp. More potent. More poignant.

Eli breathes beside me, the first inhale I've heard him take. His hands wrap around mine, and I realize I've made them into fists. He moves slowly behind me, enveloping me in his arms. In his care. In his reassurance, entirely unspoken, that no matter what happens on that table, the woman trying to take this journey will be held. Will be caught. Will be loved, whether she cracks or melts or can't find her way to either.

I can feel the tears pushing hot into my eyes, clogging my throat. This isn't theater. It's absolutely real and it's stunningly beautiful.

One more drop, and this time, whatever is building breaks through the straps inside the woman, the ones we can't see, and sets her free. Her soft moan is one of complete surrender. The candle pours a waterfall of wax, straight onto the sensitive skin between her legs, and I bear witness to the quietest, most intense orgasm I have ever seen. One so strong it turns my legs to goo.

Eli has me, holding me up and moving me away. I can see the other watchers making haste to leave too, and that feels wrong somehow. An abrupt end to the sacred, for us and for her.

Eli feels my hesitation. "Her Dom asked us to leave. He knows she won't want eyes on her now that she's come apart."

I missed the signal, whatever it was. It doesn't matter. I'm carrying the echoes of her surrender with me as I walk. I lean into Eli's strength. The desire to feel held is blazing inside me right now, but I don't know if it's truly my need or echoes of the artistry I just watched.

Eli asks me no questions. He merely guides me to the edge of yet another small gathering of people.

Chapter Twenty-Nine

ELI

She's lost the clean, clear edges of Chloe Virdani.

I know this, and I know she wants nothing more than to sit in a quiet corner and let what she just saw work its way through her as she climbs back into her own skin. Part of me is tempted to let her, because there's also a storm brewing inside of me. A wild, hopeful, grateful one, because I just got my first look at the sub that might live in the heart of the woman I love.

Or at the Domme she wants to be. Her eyes spent as much time looking at the man holding the candle as they did at the woman he was tormenting.

I take a breath. She saw the beauty of what they were together, and that's enough to earn her a place in my world. Whether she wants to enter and who she might want to be if she does are questions I don't know the answer to yet, and the storms inside me will just have to wait until I know. Until she knows. Being a Dom can be the most patience-demanding job in the universe.

I let my attention shift to what is outside me. In the last scene, Chloe saw arrows lighting the pathway to her own surrender. This one is meant to let her see if the arrows on another path burn brighter.

I guide us toward a loveseat, one that Ari has kindly arranged for the guest of honor. I catch Tamelia watching us, and do my best to signal her to take a good read of the woman at my side. The wax play has untethered Chloe, and that might impact what happens next, or at least how she perceives it.

Tamelia nods and says a few quiet words to the man perched on the edge of a stool, blindfolded and ball-gagged. He shakes his head, and she removes the gag, touching his cheek. A Domme who can't stop pushing boundaries, even when this scene is mostly for the benefit of one of its viewers. I don't know Martin well, but I know it's a victory he let her put the gag on at all.

Tamelia turns to her second sub, a young woman sitting back to back with Martin and casting interested glances at Chloe. One word from the woman in the latex pants and she pales, eyes heading straight for the floor.

A quiet chuckle from beside me. Chloe, appreciating the theater. Well on her way back into her skin.

Tamelia hasn't missed that either. She gives Chloe an assessing look as she holds up a mess of thick, clanky chains, and then her attention is entirely back on her two subs. Which is a good thing, because they're both reacting in spades. Martin is relaxing, already headed to subspace. The young woman, who I don't know, is fidgeting hard enough that she's going to dump both of them off the small stool they share.

One sub who enjoys bondage, and one who very much doesn't, but wants this badly enough to be willing to try. Tamelia has a reputation for wringing her people dry—and for building a bonfire of confidence inside them while she does.

Chloe's eyes follow the chains, fascinated, as Tamelia wraps her two scene partners up into something that looks like it belongs in a prison holding cell—one where they think Martin might turn into a werewolf any minute. Ambience. Tamelia is famous for it.

She finishes her cuffs-and-chains artwork and pulls a blind-fold down over the young woman's eyes. Her satisfied hum as the nervous sub finally quiets is audible, which isn't an accident.

And is echoed by the woman sitting beside me.

Chloe, resonating with what she sees. I hold my body still, determined to be the Dom she needs in this moment, even though I want to kick this scene in the knees or find a Domme with less-fascinating skills to finish it out. Neither of which would be remotely fair to Chloe. I take her hand instead, stroking her palm in my lap. A distraction for me, and a way to help me hang on to whatever patience I have left. There's more noise in the audience now, so I lean over and find Chloe's ear. "Any questions?"

She nods slowly. "Why the blindfolds?"

I grit my teeth and give her the answer a Domme would want to hear. "It takes away one of the ways a sub can hold themselves steady. It encourages them to lean on the steadiness the top is providing."

"It's scarier for him," Chloe says softly. "But not for her. The blindfold soothed her."

I blink. She's talking about Tamelia's two subs. "Some subs find the limited sensory input to be comforting. They like knowing someone else is firmly in charge of their experience."

Chloe's eyes are on Martin now. "Not him."

Not him at all. "It took him a lot of time and work with Tamelia to get to this point." I don't like the point I'm making, even as I make it. "Sometimes surrender is really hard."

Chapter Thirty

CHLOE

This scene is bothering Eli, and I don't think it has anything to do with chains and blindfolds. I let myself touch the discomfort and the commitment of the man standing beside me and carefully giving me the space he said he wouldn't. Steadfast space. He'll catch me in an instant if I ask him to.

I breathe in and remember Quint's words. I'm strong enough to do this with Eli standing beside me. And no matter what he's feeling, he's the one who set this scene up so that I could watch.

I know why. He thinks I might be like Tamelia. Everyone does.

I exhale and start taking inventory of my own soul.

My brain is fascinated. What's happening on that stool is a hot mix of therapy and theater and sex, and the part of me that loves understanding motivations is captivated. So is the part of me that loves bringing people into brave new worlds—I just do it with silk and lace and a well-fitting corset.

Tamelia runs a feather down the arm of one sub and they both quiver.

I smile. Her sense of timing is exquisite. She's anchoring

them to each other in every way possible, these two people with very different strengths and very different fears. I'm watching a maestro at work—even as new to this as I am, I can already see that.

I shift my focus, and this time I don't watch the woman with really excellent custom-made latex pants and fierce compassion in her eyes. I watch the two on the stool. Their shaking. The raw honesty on their faces, in their fingers, in the quiet whimpers and rasping breaths. Readying to go wherever Tamelia tells them to go.

My muscles tense in empathy with their bravery.

I close my eyes as the message of my own body sinks in. I've done the easy part. Now it's time to do the hard one. It's time to get out of my head and do the very real thing I came here to do and let myself do a walkthrough of this scene that Eli is causing himself pain to allow me to watch.

I take a quick breath and mentally launch myself out of my own skin. I head straight for a landing in Tamelia's mile-high boots and wrap myself in her utterly focused, supremely confident self-assurance. I can feel the way she assesses and measures, the quick mental rummaging through her bag of tricks as she lays out the next steps, the alternatives if things go awry. An intricate dance, one where she weaves her intentions and her arrogance together with what unfolds between the three of them.

A dance that she loves.

A reverence for the partners who are letting her lead.

I let my body feel everything about this role. It doesn't really matter whether I'm right about Tamelia. It matters that this is how I would play her, what I would feel if this were my scene and those were my partners and this was my dance.

I take one last deep breath and then I sigh quietly and step out of the mile-high boots. My body has what it came to collect. There's more to see, but I have nowhere left to put it. I need time. Time to spread out all of what has just landed in me and let it vibrate and speak and reshape itself until it fits back inside my skin and lets me be Chloe Virdani again. And I can't do that here.

I turn to the man beside me, the one whose gaze hasn't left me since Tamelia picked up her chains. "I know you asked me to let you set the pace tonight."

His whole Dom being snaps to attention. He studies me, in that way that says he's seeing all my underthings whether I want him to or not. Finally, he reaches out and run his knuckles down my cheek. "Let's go get a drink and find a couch and have a talk."

That's not what I need. I need space, unending vast expanses of it. The kind that comes with no questions and no corset laces and nothing that even kind of smells like control.

Oh, yes. Tonight has thoroughly stomped on my most sensitive buttons—and called to them. And until I know what to do with that, I feel like a ticking bomb in Eli's presence. "I need to go."

The hurt in his eyes gets whisked away in an instant—but I don't miss it.

He takes both my hands. "I can't let you do that, shorty. It's one of the rules of my world. Intense experiences need after-care. I'll let you go once I know you're okay."

It's a good rule. I'm sure it is, even if it feels like a barbed-wire fence right now. But that's not what convinces me to stay. It's knowing how much of him I would have to break through to leave. I agreed to let him hold me tonight.

I need to wait until he's ready to let me go.

Chapter Thirty-One

ELI

I've fucked up. She turned to me cracked wide open and I somehow forgot that what she needs when she's in that volcanic place is space and time to let her lava flow and make its way to the cool waters of the sea.

Instead, I stuffed her back into a bottle.

Major Dom blunder. One I can't undo, because that's not how volcanoes work. All I can do is try to fix it.

Chloe is back to her professionally curious self by the time we sit down on a quiet loveseat in the corner of the lounge. She holds a martini glass of something appropriately named Sam's Pink Disaster in one hand, and reaches for my fingers with the other.

Comforting me, and making an unspoken demand to be back on equal footing.

I sigh. I already screwed this up once, and anyone who can pull herself together this fast after what she just let herself go through doesn't need a Dom riding her ass. I take a seat beside her, sip from my own glass, which is not pink because Meghan's a smart bartender, and wait.

"That was interesting." Chloe gives me a small smile and sets her drink down.

That's a really boring word for what just happened. "Tell me about your experience." I might not feel like much of a Dom right now, but I can at least remember my lines.

Her eyes drift, tracking back through the last hour. "I like Tank and Eva a lot, but I don't understand why two people who like each other that much want to be on either end of what they were doing." She holds up a hand. "I don't need you to tell me they wanted it—I could see that. Her maybe more than him. But I could feel in my body that I don't want to be her."

I try to shift my brain back to the one scene in there I barely remember. "The story of BDSM in the vanilla world is pretty attached to impact play, but in here, there are lots of people who only dabble, or steer away from it entirely." Sometimes toward stuff she doesn't even know exists, but that's a conversation for a different day.

She nods, and then one side of her mouth tips up into a wry grin. "How long did it take before Tank figured out that she's just yelling for fun?"

Long enough to cost the poor man almost every nerve he has. "She pushed on him pretty hard. Which is a good thing. A Dom can't be tentative, and he's a big man who was scared of his own strength when he first came here."

Chloe picks up her pink martini and takes a thoughtful sip. "He'd never hurt her."

I laugh. "Listen when they come back in here. She'll try to convince everyone he nearly killed her." And in doing so, lay yet another brick onto the wall of Tank's growing self-confidence. Something Chloe clearly got, even if the impact play made her wince.

She swirls the liquid in her glass, and I can feel her energy swirling along with her drink. "The wax play was different. They weren't putting on a show."

They were, but I know what she's trying to say. "That was an intense scene for a public space."

Chloe's fingers trail along the hem of her dress, the only sign I have that she's beginning to leak out of the bottle. "Why did she freeze up?"

Good question. Brave question. "Why do you think?"

Her forehead wrinkles, and I can see the lava, pushing its way up. "It wasn't the restraints. It was almost like she was resisting the orgasm."

Smart woman. Brave woman. "She was."

She looks at me, and the entire volcano flows into her eyes. "Why?"

She knows. I know that she knows. But she needs me to say it, and I'm not going to pull out the Dom rulebook and make a second huge mistake. "Because she didn't have a choice. He was making her come."

Chloe's breath catches. "Taking the last of her control away."

I offer the counterpoint, as gently as I can. "And offering her pleasure and a chance to know herself more deeply in exchange."

Chloe's eyes have gone somewhere very far away. "He drove a very hard bargain."

"For that sub, yes." Tamelia's young woman would have given over her pleasure in a heartbeat. "Everyone has different lines that are hard for them to cross."

Chloe is quiet for a long time. "I think that would be one of mine."

I hold my breath, her words so very fragile in the air between us.

And then I do what I should have done the moment we

left the dungeon. I lean over and kiss her cheek. "Go, shorty. Take the time and the space that you need." I lean my forehead against hers, willing my shit to stay together just a little bit longer. "Thank you for trusting me tonight."

She exhales sharply, a volcano venting in relief.

I touch my fingers to her cheek. "Can I walk you home?"

She shakes her head. "No, thank you. I'll take a cab." And then she stands up, on steady legs, and walks out of my club.

Chapter Thirty-Two

CHLOE

Another bride, totally out of control. I know that as soon as I walk into my store. They very rarely escape Mandy's velvet touch, but when they do, it tends to be epic. This one has an older version of herself in tow as she stomps through our carefully manicured displays, muttering a string of curses about our monstrously erroneous sizing.

I sigh. We go down this road at least twice a week, and it's often the place where brides breach Mandy's sandbanks. She doesn't like to speak truth to curves. Or twigs, because tiny brides are just as prone to this particular display of insanity. In this case, however, the bride is straight out of a Botticelli painting, and absolutely certain a size ten is what she needs to look her wedding-night best.

Mandy looks ready to cry, which means I arrived ten minutes too late, but that can't be helped. I needed bacon and time to think. I discreetly bury the two coffees I walked in with behind a pile of lace and walk over to my assistant, using the lines of my body to begin to lay the riverbanks of calm. "I'm so sorry I'm late." I eye the mother of the bride, who looks almost as enraged as her daughter, which probably means she created this problem. "Mandy, why don't you take Clarissa and fetch us some coffee?" I'm glad I took a quick look at our appointment book on the way over—names are power.

My assistant's sigh of relief can probably be heard on the Canadian border.

Clarissa is not so easily swayed. "We don't have a lot of time this morning, and I'm not sure your shop will meet our needs."

I head around the snotty attitude and straight to what usually works. "She'll have my undivided attention while you're gone. The place across the street has the best barista in town, and you'll know just how your daughter likes her coffee."

Mandy takes Clarissa's arm, already chattering, delighted to have a script she knows how to follow. I'm not sure the mother of the bride is entirely pleased to be taken out of the picture, but she's going. Which gives me about fifteen minutes to get this train wreck back on the tracks. I look over at my Botticelli bride, who should never have been named Tiffany. "Now. Let's see what we have that will make you feel like the absolutely beautiful woman you are."

That gets rid of some of the rage—and under it, I can see the shame. "I've been working really hard to fit into my wedding dress, and everything Mandy brought me in my size doesn't fit at all."

That's not on us. A couple of the bridal shops in town are prone to sewing tags with entirely imaginary sizing into their dresses. I wish they could see the harm they do. I lead Tiffany over to a chair and sit down facing her. "I'm going to tell you something really important, all right? I need you to listen."

That gets her attention.

"The problem here isn't our sizing. It's that you don't know just how beautiful you are, and just how little that has to do with the size on the tag."

Tiffany isn't going down easily. "I'm a size ten."

Only if she plans on resembling a sausage on her wedding night. "You can keep saying that and walk out of here with something that doesn't fit and will feel tight and awful on your special day, or you can let us make you shine in the size you are. Your choice."

She stares at me, as well she should. Very few people in retail are this obnoxiously blunt.

Everyone at Fettered is.

The thought creeps in before I'm fully aware of it. Bringing my unfinished thinking over bacon into the one place it really shouldn't be. I stand up, because Tiffany needs this show to stay on the road, even though I'm feeling uncomfortably like I've stepped into a tableau from last night. Tamelia would know exactly what to do with a curvy bride trapped in a cage of her own making. "I'll go find some things I think will look spectacular on you." I wait until Tiffany meets my gaze. "You can read the tags, or you can just try them on and trust my judgment."

She nods, wide-eyed, and the similarities to last night strengthen.

I turn away. I don't go far. I scoop up a design in red that was built for curves. I can find Tiffany other options if this doesn't work, but after twenty years in this business, I'm rarely wrong.

I hear a strangled squeak behind me. "I can't wear that— it's totally see-through."

The lacy bodice is, and it's attached to a long, flowing skirt that will make her feel like a siren queen. "This lace is my own personal favorite to wear. It's stretchy and supportive and it will tease your fiancé until you decide to give him permission to touch." I hand the hanger to Tiffany and hide a grin as she carefully ignores the tag.

I can see her need to stay covered up warring with her deep attraction to the gorgeous red creation in her hands. I let the fight happen. If she can't step in to who her curves could let her be, I'll know soon enough.

Her next exhale sounds like a hot air balloon deflating. "I'll try it on."

I hear the fear and the loathing—and the fervent hope. I pull the curtain shut behind her. One more drop of molten wax, tracing a path to where she needs to go.

I hear success before I see it. The hushed, stunned, disbelieving gasp of a woman who has just looked in the mirror and dared to let herself see. I pull the curtain aside, because I live for these moments. Tiffany stares into the mirror, barely noticing me. Breathing into red lace and wonder.

A woman standing on the beautiful, fierce, trembling edges of who she is.

I shiver as my bacon-laced questions of this morning land smack in the middle of my dressing room. I'm fascinated by the Doms of Fettered. I know why they do what they do, and in this part of my life, I'm very much one of them. That would be the easy answer—but the quivers of my own skin say it might not be the right one. The harder, much scarier possibility lives in the brightness shining in Tiffany's eyes.

I might want someone to hand me red lace and bring me to the edges of who I am.

Chapter Thirty-Three
ELI

I pull my bow across the strings, letting the vibrato in my fingers give my shakiness an outlet. Or at least that's the story I'm telling myself. Mostly, I'm doing what I always do when the emotions inside me need to find some structure.

I've pulled out the big guns. This cello never leaves my home—heck, it rarely leaves my bedroom. It's the one I learned on. Not my first beginner instrument, which was only slightly better than a banana strung with elastics, but the one my parents somehow found the money for when the old Hungarian guy who was giving me lessons after school said I needed a real cello to play.

I've always imagined that it holds the echoes of most of the important moments in my life. The one where I drew a bow across its strings for the first time and realized magic lived here. The day I knew I was different and needed to get out if I wanted to keep breathing. The random afternoon when my cello sat in the corner as I gaped at the vision of teenage wonderfulness that had just walked into the student lounge, taken a seat beside me, and started talking.

Chloe carried on that conversation without much help from me for the better part of an hour.

The cello laughs under my hands. It has born witness to so very many awkward Eli moments.

I let the piece I'm fiddling with morph into something lighter. Something less angsty, with more room for laughter and compassion and thought. I don't want to be this much of a mess when Chloe finds me again. And I want to make sure I've mined all the richness of what she let me see last night.

I let my fingers wander as I make a mental list. Bondage is high on her interest meter. The tight, very thorough kind. Impact play is likely a lost cause, although no Dom worth his salt would take that as a final answer. It didn't move her, though—not in any direction that leads to arousal. But easily the most fascinating part of watching Chloe last night was seeing someone entirely new to my world read deep into the head game of kink. She saw so many of the layers. Understood them.

My bow scratches and makes me wince. Saying what I don't want to.

She'd make a really good Domme.

Except I'm not sure that's what I saw last night either. I drop my bow and pick my fingers across the strings, pizzicato accompaniment to the frustration of pieces I still can't align. Chloe was intrigued by the psychology of kink, but her deepest moments last night were ones I would expect from a sub. One who might have a wish for utter and complete surrender—the kind that needs to be tied down and chased out with fire.

Or I'm a Dom with a bad case of wish fulfillment.

My cello sings my own ridiculousness back to me. I shake my head and make a face at the instrument that's dealt with so much of my angst over the years and managed to keep a sense of humor. I pick my bow back up off the floor and play a few bars of Mozart. The structure and framing of classical music has always soothed us both.

All those music lessons probably laid the foundation that made me a Dom. Or both were simply a recognition of something foundational in who I've been since the day I was born.

I sigh and close my eyes, knowing I've arrived at the crux.

I'm asking Chloe to consider if she's kinky. To consider revamping the entire foundation of who she is as a sexual being. I'm sitting here considering asking the same of myself, even though I know the answer. I can feel what could be with Chloe, and it's so very tempting to lop off the corners of who I am to make it work. But I remember the bone-deep recognition the first time I walked into a club. The fierce glow that lit in my belly the first time a sub truly surrendered in my care.

Giving it up would be as hard, and as damaging, and as wrong, as giving up my music.

Sitting here in the light of day with my cello, I can be honest enough to say that pisses me off. I wish kink felt like optional wiring, like a part of me I could unplug and stick into any old outlet and have it still work. Or even a really great outlet—vanilla sex with Chloe is freaking awesome, and there's so much more there.

But there isn't space for all of who I am.

I realize that I'm not playing Mozart anymore. What I am playing is ragged and raw and beautiful. And old. It's the first piece I ever composed, back on the day that Chloe sent me away to go be all of who I was meant to be.

Even if that meant I couldn't be hers.

I close my eyes and let the strength of that flow into my fingers. She was riverbanks for me back then, and I need to honor that. To give her space to make her own choices, even if her wiring doesn't end up any more flexible than mine.

I let those words sit a minute, and then I snort. I've caught a bad case of teenage melancholy from my cello. To hell with space. She absolutely needs to make her own choices, but I'm a Dom, and I don't do riverbanks from afar.

I lean my cello against the wall and pick up my phone. I've given her space. An entire half-day of it. Now it's time to try a little immersion.

Chapter Thirty-Four

CHLOE

I look down at the package in my hands, aware that they're shaking. The text from Eli didn't help. Time isn't standing still while I figure this out. I take a breath. Knowing something in the comfort of my own shop and holding on to it out here in the big, scary world are two very different things.

The door in front of me opens, and a very smart pair of eyes surveys my face—and my package. Ari grins and reaches for the shiny wrapped present like a toddler on her birthday. "Is that for me?"

I laugh. "It is."

She rips into Mandy's careful wrapping job, pulls out a deep-blue velvet corset and matching mini-skirt, and makes a sound that's most of the way to thoroughly delighted orgasm.

I make a note to let the man who sewed it together deliver it next time. He thrives on being appreciated.

Ari holds up the corset by a slinky strap, pleasure all over her face. "One of your new designs?"

Probably. "Consider it a gift to a really great business partner." She's been wonderful, and I've never stinted on thanking the people who make my world better.

Her grin goes goopy—and then her eyes sharpen and give me a thorough once-over. "This isn't the only reason you came."

Busted, and I didn't even make it through the door. "I was hoping to talk to you." I wince, because the next part sucks, but I'm not sure how to get around it. "Or to have you point me in the direction of someone else I can talk to if you're uncomfortable mixing business with the inner workings of my sex life."

The giggle that squirts out of her goes a long way to setting my mind at ease. "Sweetie, the inner workings of everyone's sex life *is* my business." She slings her hand through my elbow. "Come on into my parlor, and I'll get us something pink to drink and chase all the nosy Doms out of the lounge so that we can talk."

There are no Doms in the lounge, which is too bad, because watching Ari boss the world around is pure fun. I take the drink she hands me and let her herd us to a cushy loveseat in the corner. I've already learned that everyone at Fettered sits close to everyone else. Touch only happens by consent, but closeness is offered easily and often.

She clinks her drink on mine. "Okay, love. Dish. What's on your mind?"

"I learned some things from my tour last night."

She nods and sips the diabetic coma in her glass. "Most people do—the honest ones, anyhow."

"You're a Domme."

Another casual sip and a nod. "Sometimes."

"I have a lot of the skills to be one."

A friendly grin. "Yup, you do."

She's not herding me at all now, even though she's more than capable, and I breathe into the space she's allowing for me to take this walk. The very jittery, nervy space. "I saw some people I didn't want to be last night, but a couple of scenes surprised me."

Her eyes are steady on mine. "Aroused you."

This is so not a conversation to be having with a business partner. "Yes." I frown, digging for what lived in my belly as I watched the falling drops of wax. "Or something beyond."

"Mira." Ari nods. "The woman in the wax play scene."

She knows. Of course she knows. I take a deep, harsh breath. "It was so hard for her, and yet I wanted to be right where she was."

"You got lucky." Ari's voice gentles, her eyes two deep-blue pools of compassion. "That sense of longing, even if you don't understand it, is an amazing mirror into who you are. Into who your insides want or maybe even need you to be."

I shake my head, nerves morphing into acute frustration. "How could I not already know that about myself?"

Ari sets down her drink and smiles. "Because sometimes this stuff sneaks up on us and bites us in the ass."

The pressure inside me lets out with a whoosh. That's exactly what it was. A total sneak attack. I'm not oblivious—I just got ambushed by my own insides. "Everyone seems to think I'd rather be the person doing the biting."

She shrugs and grins. "Some of us are born to be one thing. Some of us aren't. You don't need me to tell you that nobody else gets to decide this for you."

I nod, feeling my way a little deeper into the ball of hard and sad that's attached to this whether I want it there or not. "Eli is one thing. He's a Dom, all the way through."

Ari hums under her breath. "Yes and no."

That's not the answer I was expecting.

"It's a spectrum. Some people are all the way to the sub end, some all the way to the Dom end, and some of us stand with one foot on each side of the teeter-totter. But there are lots of other flavors." She hums again and glances at her phone. "Which I could tell you about, but it would be way better for you to see for yourself. Ready for another tour?"

I raise an eyebrow. She's herding again, and I don't know where.

She stands up and pulls me to my feet. "Sam's making tacos tonight."

That much I know. "Eli sent me a text."

Her lips quirk. "Did he now? Pushy Dom."

Says the person who was already planning on shoving me in that particular direction. I grin at her. "Pushy switch."

"Totally." She smirks and drops our drinks on the bar. "Their place is just a few blocks away. It will be the perfect chance for you to see kinky relationships in the wild."

I scramble to keep up. "And that's the thing I need to do right now because...?"

She's already halfway out the door. "Because Soleil is the cutest baby in the history of the universe. And because you need to see how people balance their needs for control and surrender outside the club."

She spins around to face me. "Last night gave you one kind of data. Before you decide what to do about that cliff you're standing on, take one more afternoon."

I stare at her. I haven't said a word about the cliff.

Her sincerity is a living thing. "I stood there once too. I remember."

Chapter Thirty-Five

ELI

The gang is literally all here. I make my way into the throngs in Sam's and Leo's back yard, letting the swell of voices and laughter and the smells of whatever's on Sam's grill wash over me. Playing the cello alone has always been one of my best forms of medicine. Tribe is the other.

I catch a bullet with arms and legs right before it crashes into my leg. Daniel skids to a stop right behind her, laughing as I hand him the streaking girl. "Evie, doll, you're going to break someone if you don't look where you're going."

She grins at him, covered in ketchup and clearly unconcerned. "He catched me."

"A girl after my own heart." Sam leans in and gives the toddler a big, smoochy kiss on the cheek. "A party's no fun until you've gotten in trouble at least once, right, sugar?"

Evie laughs. Daniel snorts. "Just wait until Soleil starts walking."

"You hush." Sam shakes his head. "We're keeping her right this size for the rest of her life."

I look around, trying to find the baby in the sea of heads. "Who's kidnapped her?"

Sam rolls his eyes. "The first person, or who has her right now?"

I imagine he could give me a list, with times and locations of each exchange. Sam is exuberant and outrageous, but he misses exactly nothing—and he adores his daughter with the wild mop of hair and the dark-eyed gaze that matches his. "You might have to search people when they leave."

Leo swings in to join us, laughing at my comment. "They'll give her back when it's nap time. Her lungs are really impressive."

Daniel backs away, listening carefully to whatever Evie's whispering into his ear. I grin at Leo. "I hear babies are really good at topping from the bottom."

Leo laughs again and wraps an arm around Sam. "They are. And she's got an excellent teacher."

Sam has a stellar wounded-innocent look. "Such accusations, and after I spent all day teaching her how to blow bubbles just for her Pops."

Leo's whole face melts. "Aww, did she finally do it?"

"Nope. She's waiting for you." This smoochy kiss is for Leo's cheek, and then we're whirlwinding again, Sam dragging me off to parts unknown. "You look hungry. Come."

I follow him as he heads to the grill. There's no evading Sam's tacos, even if I wanted to.

He plucks Soleil out of Mattie's arms on the way. She just grins and spanks his ass. I shake my head and give her a wry look. Apparently I'm not the only one who struggles with the rules for vanilla behavior.

Sam stops at the grill and snuggles his baby girl under his chin. "What do you think, wiggle bug? Should we feed Uncle Eli the spicy tacos today, or the extra-special body-slam version?"

I hope Soleil knows that my stomach lining is white, Jewish, and a little touchy about being set on fire.

Sam winks at his daughter, picks up a bottle of something hot and red, and squirts it liberally onto the spoonful of meat already sitting on a soft taco shell.

I don't ask. I watch Soleil's droopy eyes instead. One baby who feels entirely safe with her daddy.

"So." Sam scoops toppings from the nearby table onto my plate, clearly not trusting me with my own taco. "Have you tied Chloe up and had your way with her yet?"

I wince. "Does my answer influence what you're going to put on that?" Sam has used his grill to get even with more than one Dom.

He laughs. "Yes. Don't lie."

I wouldn't have anyhow. "No. She has to choose this freely. Not everyone is meant to be kinky." No matter how much pressure my inner Dom would like to apply.

Soleil chooses that moment to let out a sleepy, fussy wail.

Sam slides her into some kind of contraption on his chest, bouncing in time to the universal beat only parents can hear. "It's okay, sweetie love. You can grow up to be straight and vanilla and your daddies will still love you."

I grin—and then it fades as I realize my answer is exactly the same as his.

I'll still love Chloe, too.

Chapter Thirty-Six

CHLOE

I sit on the swinging bench in the back corner of Sam's yard, cuddling a sleepy girl who didn't even introduce herself before she crawled into my lap. I can tell from the envious glances being cast my way that I somehow drew one of the really lucky straws.

And it's giving me a chance to watch. To observe. To see what kinky relationships look like in the wild. Because Ari wasn't wrong. The flavors could fill a whole ice-cream shop. Gabby, wiping crumbs off Daniel's face and walking away swishing her hips, entirely ignoring the evil glint in his eye. Scorpio, who I've mostly seen owning the heck out of her stage, all soft-eyed and goopy and tucking into Harlan's side when he arrived like he was everything good in her world. Quint, wearing a sexy apron I'm absolutely sure isn't his and growling at Meghan as they keep everyone supplied with a rainbow of frothy, tasty drinks.

I see so many things here I could be. So many ways I could walk with Eli through the taco barbecues of our lives. Life on the other side of the cliff wouldn't be the problem. Which leaves me sitting here staring straight at the hard and scary, completely stripped naked of any excuses I might have tried to cover it up with.

And left holding one daunting, damning realization.

The cliff isn't what I thought it was. This isn't about what Eli might ask of me and what I might be willing to do to walk at his side. It might have started off there, but that changed the moment I stood in his dungeon, my eyes glued to drops of falling wax, and heard glaciers crack.

When I look around this back yard, the one thing I don't see is glaciers. I don't know who here is like me, who looks at the cliff of their own surrender and wonders if it might be the hardest thing they've ever done, who here doesn't want the cliff but thinks they might need it.

But I know they all got through it the very same way. Just like the small girl in my lap.

They were held.

Chapter Thirty-Seven

ELI

She's been sitting there for more than an hour, swinging gently, with Evie's far more sedate twin cuddled in her lap.

Nothing else about what is happening on that swing is gentle. I've seen subs on precipices before, and this one has spent the last hour crumbling under Chloe's feet. On purpose. A wildly courageous journey, and she's doing it without a Dom. Without any safewords. Without a safety net.

Not because she couldn't have one if she wanted. There are at least a dozen people currently prowling her periphery waiting for permission, and all of them would have to plant me six feet underground first. But Chloe hasn't asked, and her words from our dinner two nights ago are seared into my brain.

I need to give up the control, not have you take it.

She hasn't given it up.

She doesn't want to—but she thinks that maybe she needs to, and she's holding her own feet to the fire in a way that has half the people in this back yard watching in admiration as she does the most important walk a sub can ever do.

Alone.

She's holding on to control by her fingernails, but she hasn't given it up. And until she does, I can't take it. I know the precipice she's on—it's written all over her face. Two days ago she needed to understand my motivation, why I do this. Today, she needs to understand her own. She's not a classic sub. She doesn't need to please. She doesn't desire to be controlled, she doesn't thrive inside structure, and she's not a brat.

But for the first time, not one person in this yard is looking at the woman I love and seeing the club's next trainee Domme. They're seeing the truth that Chloe is grappling with in the pit of her very naked soul. The part of her that might not desire or want or crave surrender—but is called to it anyhow.

A hand clamps on my shoulder. Quint, helping me hold still a few seconds longer.

"I have to wait." My voice sounds like I've been shouting for three days.

"Yeah." He watches Chloe, his eyes full of respect. "If she makes the leap, she's going to be amazing."

Yes. *If*.

He finally looks at me. "And she's going to be a hell of a challenge. She'll have to trust her Dom a lot."

That may be the only thing keeping me sane. "She already does."

He squeezes my shoulder. "Not for this."

My growl comes out more like a whimper. "Did you come over here to help or to drive me crazy?"

He snorts, but his hand on my shoulder says something different. He didn't come over to do either. He came to be a friend. One who knows what it is to hold his own demons still while the woman he loves grapples with hers.

Chapter Thirty-Eight

CHLOE

I'm full again, even though all I've eaten is taco fumes—and I need to think. But first I need to finish a conversation that started before I got here.

Ari sees me coming and gracefully extracts from her collection of adoring admirers, little and big. She gives me a hug, the kind that says she sees all my confused pieces and honors them. "Got all the data you need?"

I shrug. "Maybe. I think so. I need some time to let it settle."

Her smile is slow and a little bit sad. "Don't take too long."

I sigh and cast a glance at Eli, who's carefully not looking at me. "Because it's hurting him to wait?"

She shakes her head. "No. Because it's hurting you."

She is so very much like me. "He thinks I'm doing this to protect him."

She studies me carefully. "Are you?"

"No. Maybe at sixteen, he needed me to protect him. He doesn't now. He needs me to figure myself out."

Ari's eyes shine with sisterhood—and respect. "You are,

and you will." She pauses a beat. "Consider letting him hold you while you do it."

Her words are the scariest thing in the world. I close my eyes. "I like being the person other people can lean on."

I hear the compassion in her voice. "Me too."

I follow the string she's laid out for me, straight over to the edge of the cliff I've been trying to convince myself isn't mine. This isn't about protecting Eli at all. It's about protecting me. About wanting to keep the glaciers of my soul right where they are. I swallow hard and ask the only question I have left. "Is it hard for you?"

She laughs quietly. "The hardest. It took me about a day to become a Domme. The sub part was a lot harder. And a lot more important."

I nod. "Thanks."

She kisses my cheek. "Anytime."

I walk over to Eli, and even though he's not looking at me, I know he feels me coming. I stop, just shy of his shoulder, and wait until he turns my way, hope and terror in his eyes.

I'm not sure enough of where I am to speak to either. "Can I come see you tomorrow?"

He takes a really long time to answer. An empty space filled with everything neither of us can say. "Yes."

I nod. I'm going to find myself a taco to eat and hug every darn person in this yard. And then I'm going to go home, pull the covers up over my head, and stare at a cliff.

Chapter Thirty-Nine

ELI

I know it's her at my door even before I open it. Nothing mystical—my ears just know the rhythm of her footsteps. I can't stop the part of me that loves that level of connection, even knowing that what's about to walk in my door might wreak havoc with the rest of me.

Watching her slip out of Sam and Leo's yard yesterday afternoon was hell. The twenty-eight hours since have been a place I didn't even know existed.

She smiles when I open up. "Hi. I'm glad you're home. I followed your neighbor in." She waves down the hall at the elderly man who lives in the condo at the far end and obviously finds Chloe charming. "Do you have some time to talk?"

I'd do surgery on my day if I didn't. On my life. "Yes." I back up so she can walk in my door, trying to read her body language. Which is about as effective as trying to stare at the zucchini in my fridge and learn where it grew. Body language needs context, and I don't have any for this conversation yet.

I do, however, have zucchini. "You hungry? I was just about to make a stir fry." Which names all the things I can cook, but fortunately stir fries come in infinite flavors.

She grins. "Still making those?"

"Yes." I tweak her nose as I turn toward my kitchen, stupidly grateful for small comforts. "Still pretending you don't know which end of a knife is the business end?"

She laughs. "I'm forty-two. I could only delay the inevitable for so long."

I wish we felt inevitable. The romantic in me wants it to be so, but the man who's been happily single for the last twenty-six years is well aware we're two people totally capable of walking away from this. Even if it turns us into emotional spaghetti.

I open my fridge and pull out all the veggies that look decent. Which includes two zucchini, some cipollini onions, and a somewhat questionable eggplant. I put the eggplant back and pull out beef strips instead. The veggies might be a little sketchy, but the tiny woman who runs the Asian market down the street and thinks I need a wife keeps me well supplied in things that stir fry with very little fuss. I reach back into the fridge for the sprouted beans and a bottle of the all-purpose sauce I use when I'm feeling lazy. Or distracted.

Chloe has already found my knife collection and is demonstrating the impressive skills she's acquired in the last twenty-six years. There's a nice mountain of zucchini toothpicks, and onion slivers coming up right behind them.

Right. I pull out a wok that might be older than I am. It's seen as many countries too, and it kept me well fed in most of them. I give it less time than I probably should to warm up and pull the lid off the rice cooker while I wait. Lots there. "Food in five minutes."

She grins and pushes a cutting board piled high with veggies my way. "Does your place run to a bottle of wine on short notice?"

I shake my head, amused at my suddenly sixteen-year-old

manners. "I spent two decades in Europe." I nod at the end of the counter. "The high-tech contraption for storing wine is under the end there. Pick any bottle you like. French on the top racks, more adventurous stuff lower down."

It doesn't surprise me in the slightest when she sticks her nose in the very bottom.

I breathe into that. The knowledge that Chloe has always been brave. The comfort of having her here, perusing my wine collection. I push the beef around, searing it in the high heat. Chloe mutters something I can't hear and emerges with a bottle. I leave her to it—I assume she's learned how to boss a cork around in the last couple of decades too.

She sets the open bottle on the counter to breathe just as I pour a cascade of chopped zucchini and onion into my wok, and sniffs appreciatively as the sauce lands a few seconds later. "That smells yummy."

I grin. "Four ingredients in a jar, and they all love beef." I kiss her forehead. "Thanks for chopping."

She leans into me, arms around my waist, hanging on lightly as I push beef and veggies around a wok and wish stir fry took a lot longer to cook. "Thanks for letting me in your door."

I kiss her forehead again. "Always." I mean it, in so very many ways I don't know how to put into words. Which, for right now, I can live with. I reach for the sprouts, which my tiny Korean shopkeeper assures me make for very virile sperm, and drop a heaping handful on top of everything else. "Cashews?"

It takes her a minute to figure out what I'm asking, which is good for my ego. She can get lost in the touch and feel of my chest any time she pleases. "Sure."

I reach for a canister and throw on some of those and a little more sauce, and then, because this is a really fancy establishment, I scoop the rice straight out of the rice cooker and into the wok. Asian grannies everywhere roll over into their graves, but I want my rice warm and I don't want to unwind from Chloe to do it.

She grins as I pile two plates high. "You don't eat it straight out of the wok anymore?"

Not when I want to hold a really sexy woman in my lap while I eat. "Chopsticks or forks?"

She gives me a dirty look. The kind that says a fork will be turned into origami along with my eyeballs.

I laugh and pull out two sets of beautiful ironwood chopsticks with cherry bark overlays that I acquired from their maker the last time my tour bus took a left turn through Japan.

Chloe hums appreciatively and runs her finger along the grain of the wood.

I hold back a growl. I know I'm in deep trouble when I'm jealous of a chopstick.

Chapter Forty

CHLOE

The chopsticks are beautiful and precise and intriguing, just as he's always chosen for his instruments. I take them, along with two glasses of wine, and head for his couch.

He gets there before me, setting down two plates and taking the wine glasses from my hands. An arm slides around my waist as he sits down, and then he's assembling me in his lap as casually and confidently as he handled the wine glasses.

He's different now. He's still the Eli who cooks stir fries and collects beautiful things made of wood, but he also has a calm, rooted self-assurance. A control that balances where he goes with his music. I let myself breathe into that. I was the one who sent him off to find musical freedom once. Maybe I'm here to ask him to complete the circle.

I hand over one set of chopsticks, somewhat reluctantly. They're beautiful, and my hands have always coveted pretty things to touch.

He picks up a mouthful of my favorite bits and offers it, the ironwood a smooth extension of his fingers.

I shiver. Even at sixteen, those fingers knew how to play me.

He chuckles. "That bad?"

I blink, and the flavors of the tangy-sweet sauce land, somewhat belatedly. "No, it's really tasty." Surprisingly so. The ingredients might be similar to the ones teenage Eli used, but he's gotten a lot better at throwing them together. I chew on beef that has just the right amount of tang to go along with the sauce, and scoop up a far more loaded bite.

He looks hopeful, and I laugh. "Feed yourself, buster. I don't have your skill with chopsticks and this is too good to be picking up off your shirt."

He smiles and nuzzles into my cheek. "It's good to have you here, shorty."

I can hear what he's not saying. It doesn't matter why I've come. We'll get through this. I take another bite and chew meditatively, trying to figure out where to start, and decide to begin at the end. "I want you to play with me. A full-blown scene. A serious one that really pushes on me."

His body doesn't react, but his chopsticks freeze in mid-air. "That's not a good choice for a beginner."

I don't care. "I'm not asking you to be my trainer. I'm asking you to help us find out what happens if you lean on me the way the Dom with the candle was leaning on his sub." I put down my plate and turn in his lap to face him. "We're not beginners to each other, Eli. I know you could give me a nice hands-on tour of kink, but that's not what I need from you. I need to know if I can fit who I am to who you are."

His eyes are sad. "That's not how it works. I don't want you to fit to me."

I shake my head, frustrated, because the words are awkward and clunky and I need them out of the way. "I don't mean it like that. I saw something in the wax play that called to me."

His eyes stay on mine. "I know."

There's that arrogance. It intrigues me, even as it makes me tremble. "I want to know, and I'm not going to know if we're just walking through a scene hitting our marks and saying our lines."

He smiles and strokes my hair. "Full dress rehearsal, huh?"

More like opening night. There are going to be so many people watching, even if we're tucked away in the privacy of his bedroom. "Yes. I need it to be deeply real, or I won't know for sure."

He nods slowly, tipping his forehead into mine. "I need you to know that what you're asking for is really dangerous territory."

I borrow a line from my sixteen-year-old self as I poke him in the ribs. "Duh."

He laughs and straightens back up, eyes twinkling. "How much does Ari have to do with you being here?"

Busted. "I went to talk with her. I put it off for a while because she's my primary business contact on the lingerie deal, but I needed to talk to someone who really gets how hard it is to be a sub."

His smile is pleased, and a little rueful. "I was going to ask her to talk to you. Was she helpful?"

I nod. "She told me it was hard. And totally worth it."

I can see the relief he's trying to hide. I lean forward, touching my cheek to his. "Can you do it? Be my Dom like that?"

He takes a minute, and I can nearly hear those calm, self-assured wheels turning. "Yes."

I back up, seeking his eyes, needing to see if the shadows are gone. "You're sure?"

His grin has a tinge of arrogance that sixteen-year-old Eli would have found totally foreign. "People tell me I'm pretty good at this."

I punch his bicep as hard as I can with only six inches to maneuver.

He laughs and cups my face in his hands. "It would be a bad idea with any two other people, but you already know that. We'll be okay. I just need one promise from you."

My stomach lurches. His words have a seriousness, a weight that doesn't match his smile. "What?"

All humor flees—and the shadows are back. Not sad ones this time. Deep, serious ones. "Whatever happens, I need you to stay after. Until we're both okay."

I swallow hard and close my eyes, even as my hands seek his, even as I lean into the warmth of his heartbeat. I know why he's asking.

We might not be okay after. We might be done.

Chapter Forty-One

ELI

Unsettling a sub before a scene is a standard Dom trick. That's not what I'm doing. She's just thoroughly unsettled me, and I need to know we'll still be here to catch each other if this runs into a brick wall. Which is such an unfair request of a sub, especially a brand-new one, that I'm pretty sure they're sending an emergency team to repossess my Dom card.

But we aren't just two people about to explore some kink together. We're Chloe and Eli and we go way back and I need to know more than anything that we're going to protect that. No kink is worth losing a piece of your heart for.

She cuddles into me in a way I don't really remember Chloe cuddling. One that's letting me feel her shivers. "Agreed."

It's not the agreement that kicks my Dom into gear—it's the shivers. She's a sub who's already doing her part and getting vulnerable, and we haven't even started yet. I lift her chin so that I can see her eyes. This is going to be the shortest negotiation in the history of short negotiations, but it still needs to happen. For her and for me. "You have your safe-words. Tell me what they are and what they mean."

Her eyes flash annoyed at the surprise quiz, and then the annoyance clears. Smart Chloe, catching on fast to why the rules exist. "Yellow to slow down, red to stop."

Yellow is more diverse than that, but it will work for today. Especially with rule number two, which is one I've never given a sub before. "I also need you to ditch the walls. If we're going to go deep, I need to be able to read you. All of you. No hiding, no protecting me, no saving things for thinking about later."

She looks at me for a long time, her quiet eyes entirely comprehending just how naked I've asked her to get. "Okay."

I can feel myself wanting to get high off that single word. For me, kink is like music—the fingering is just the path to the emotions. But I can't feel yet. I have a sub still in her packaging who is waiting for me to do something wondrous. I stroke my hand down her hair, mentally matching up what I know from watching her in the dungeon with tools I can lay my hands on in my condo on very short notice. I need bondage, and lots of it. The rest I can make up as I go.

I move my hands to her waist, intending to send her to my bedroom, when I spy my cello, case open, sitting in the corner. And feel my first plan jumping headlong out the window as a scene floods into my head, fully formed.

Fully formed—and the most intimate, scary thing I've ever contemplated doing as a Dom.

She feels my stutter, but I leave it hanging between us. This is too big to rush. Too big for her to walk in believing I'm totally certain. It's also entirely right. A scene that will offer her every bit of who I am, streamed through a medium that just might help me keep my shit together. A scene that could only be hers and mine.

Chloe and Eli as we might be.

Chapter Forty-Two

CHLOE

Whatever hit Eli's pause button is done. I see it in his eyes before I feel it in his hands. The guy who took me on a tour of the dungeon two nights ago has just showed up.

I will myself to let this happen.

He sets his hands on my hips. "Strip, shorty."

I can feel my eyes goggling. That's so not where I expected this to start. I'm not sure why—every sub I saw in the dungeon was close to naked. I swallow, deeply feeling the psychology of why.

He doesn't say anything more. He just looks at me. Expecting obedience.

I can feel the urge to kick his knees coming in for a landing. I push it away. That's not who I want to be today. I know, right down to the very heart of me, that Eli would never do anything to make me less.

This is his first drop of candle wax.

I wrap my hands around each other, trying to stop their trembling, and I stand. I leave the warm comfort of his lap for the stark reality of standing on my own two feet and taking off all the layers I use to cover me.

Undressing has never felt quite so stark.

He watches me, his eyes never wavering from that calm sternness. I want to believe it's reassuring, but nothing in me feels that way. I asked him to push. To make this real. He's letting me see his answer.

I gulp and look away, letting my pants fall to my ankles. I leave the scraps of deep-green lace where they are. He'll know it's my armor, but I need it for a little while longer. I unbutton the silky shirt I picked up at a market in Nepal. My version of Eli's chopsticks. It falls to the floor beside my pants, and I realize I'm standing in my underwear—with my shoes still on and my pants around my ankles holding me captive.

I've had better planning days.

I shake my head wryly and sit down on a footstool to rectify my mistake. I glance at Eli, but there's nothing showing in his eyes. Not even amusement, and there's no way he isn't finding this funny. Which means there's purpose to his poker face. More drops of wax.

I manage to get my shoes and pants off like an actual grown-up and stand back up. I love this green silk bra, and I want him to get a good look before he makes me take it off.

This time, amusement glints in his eyes before he lifts an eyebrow. "Those too."

I figured. I reach around behind me for the clasp of the bra. It's one of my designs, but that isn't helping my shaking fingers get the job done. I pause and gulp. This is just another stage. Another performance. I can do this. I somehow finagle the clasp and let the straps slide down my arms. This is the least sexy strip-tease ever, but we both know that teasing isn't its purpose. Everything about this feels deadly serious.

I hook my fingers inside the lace over my hips and pause. Not to resist—to fully feel this moment. I look at Eli, at his watchful eyes taking in all of me. Not in a way that wants, although somehow I'm in no doubt at all that he does. This is something deeper. Something that needs to come first. Something that will turn wanting into an emotion far stronger.

I feel every molecule of lace as it slides down the skin of my thighs, dusting to the floor. Leaving me as naked as I've ever been—because we both know I just took off a whole lot more than clothes.

Chapter Forty-Three

ELI

She's so gorgeous, and full of awareness that new subs almost never have. A woman who could easily be a Domme and is choosing something else. I'd be asking her a lot of hard questions about that, except I felt her breathe beside me as she watched the wax play.

I felt her yearn.

I stand up and pull the end of my brown leather chaise away from the wall. It's a handy piece of furniture, well padded with no back and only a low armrest. Excellent for playing the cello and other nefarious uses, although I only realized the latter about three minutes ago. I eyeball the angles. I want no distractions in this scene, at least not the kind that come from knees and elbows accidentally meeting drywall. I walk around my living area, picking up an armful of the fat pillows my very vanilla interior designer insisted were necessary to my wellbeing.

Today, she's absolutely right.

I keep my movements slow, deliberate. Sliding the basic Dom scaffolding into place. I control the clothing. I control the furniture. I control the timing.

I walk back over to the end of the chaise and make two stacks of two pillows each. Then, still crouched down, I motion to Chloe, who's tracking me with watchful, curious eyes.

I'm about to add anxious to that mix.

I pat the arm rest. "Bend over, ass in the air, knees on the pillows."

She stares at me.

It takes every ounce of willpower I've developed in the last twenty-six years not to grin. "Now, Chloe."

My voice gets her feet going, which soothes my Dom nerves. She may not look like a sub, she may not act like a sub —but if Dom voice works on the woman I love, then she's got at least some wiring that goes along with her desire to be pushed into surrender. I stand as she approaches the chaise, moving the power from my voice into my stance.

Her breath is catching in her throat, little panting gasps that are like no sound I've ever heard from her. I check in with the rest of her body. She's not aroused yet—but she's not far away.

The next part will either get her there or convince her this is the worst idea she's ever had.

I arrange the pillows under her knees. I want her comfortable—she's going to be here for a while. The chaise nicely tips her ass up without putting too much of a curve in her spine. I move her limbs, reposition her head, using touch to soothe and arrange. Letting her get a feel for having someone else entirely in charge of something as simple as where her arms rest and where her hair lies. I'm tempted to leave it in a tumble down her back, but that's a really poor idea with what's coming next. I stroke her cheek. "I'll be right back. I need to gather some things."

She's dazed enough she doesn't protest.

I walk slowly until I'm out of her line of sight, and then I burn rubber, because leaving a newbie sub alone is the height of stupid. However, it's a necessary stupid. Chopsticks don't offer many bondage options. Fortunately, my closet does. I grab a bag, still packed from the demo I did at Fettered a couple of weeks back, and mentally run through the contents. I dive into a second bag and pull out a small collection of toys for sensory play. I don't do candles, so that part of this scene is going to be very much winging it.

Assuming I get back to the couch before my sub totally wigs out.

I nearly run to the corner of the hall and then resume my measured pace as I reenter Chloe's realm.

Her eyes widen as she catches sight of the black bags in my hands. I drop them at the edge of the chaise, down below what she can see. Good for easy access, and good for frustrating someone who likes to have all the information. Protest rises in her eyes, but she manages to lock it back down.

A sub already wise enough to be restraining herself.

I reach into my bag for the long, soft strips of leather that can be adapted to almost any bondage setup. Some Doms like precision tools. I prefer flexibility. The legacy of spending a lot of years playing in a different city every week. I hold up the balled leather straps where Chloe can see them.

This time her eyes don't widen. They glow.

I stroke a hand down her back. There are things she needs to hear before I shut down her words. "If you get scared, if you get a cramp, if you get an itch between your shoulder blades, I need to hear about it." That's more latitude than I would normally give a sub, but it's the only way I know to keep dangerous and new from turning into catastrophe.

She nods quietly.

I hold on to the end of one of the balls and drop the rest

over the side edge of the chaise, grinning when it cooperatively rolls out from underneath. I haven't lost my touch—or I have sloping floors. Either way, I'm going to be able to get this done without floundering around on the floor, which isn't the Dom image I'm shooting for right now.

I have balls two and three rolled out under the chaise before Chloe's eyes get any more focus back. I reach for my shorter straps. We'll start with the parts that are easiest to adapt. Wanting to be tied up and handling the actual experience of forced immobility are two very different things, and I need to let Chloe tiptoe in before I toss her headlong into the deep end she's asked for.

Chapter Forty-Four

CHLOE

He's going to tie me up. My brain knows it and my gut knows it and apparently whatever makes little goosebumps stand up all over my body knows it.

He reaches for my wrist, looping an incredibly soft, wide band of leather around my forearm all the way down to my wrist. He leaves the tail of the leather hanging and does the same to my other arm. I'm in some kind of daze where I'm letting him move me around like a puppeteer's doll. Then he bends down, and I can feel him attaching the ends of the straps to something I can't see. Chair legs, maybe. It doesn't matter. Theater doesn't always get better when you look behind the curtain.

He attaches a short strap to one wrist and runs it carefully under my chest, tying it to my other wrist, far enough apart that my hands can lie comfortably by my shoulders. I tug. Attached, but I have plenty of range of motion.

Which, to my utter astonishment, makes me more than a little grumpy.

Eli chuckles as he does something with another strap, closer to my feet this time, and suddenly I'm trussed like a turkey, or like a turkey would be if it had arms. In one swift move, he's performed some kind of kinky magical act and rendered my hands entirely stuck. Nothing is tight, nothing hurts—but I can move my arms all of a finger-width in any direction.

I can feel his eyes on me. Studying, making sure I'm all right.

I'm not sure I want to be, but that small grumpy voice has entirely shut up. I shift my head a little and settle in.

His hand strokes down my back, over my bare ass. I figure out what's coming next just before the strap of leather winds around my left thigh. Just like with my arm, he goes around several times. Unlike with my arm, that takes his hands notably closer to parts of me that are starting to pay fluttery attention.

I squeeze my eyes shut. Just getting tied up shouldn't be arousing.

Same action on my other thigh, and then light fingers trace circles over the curves of my ass. "Comfortable?"

I try to move my legs and discover I've become part of the chaise. I'm not going anywhere. I tug again, not at all sure how I feel about this.

His head drops down by my ear. "I need your words, Chloe. Is anything uncomfortable? Binding you too tightly?"

Not physically. I make a face. "No. But I don't know if I like this."

A low, gravelly chuckle. "That's not what I asked you."

I growl. "It's what I wanted to say."

A hand lands sharply on my ass, and it hurts. "Respect the process and respect your Dom, or we're done."

The burning sensation on my ass is nothing compared to the one in my brain—the one processing that gentle, sensitive Eli has just hit me.

His breath whispers past my ear again. "You have your safewords."

I've never underestimated the color red, but right now it feels like bringing a bubble wand to a grenade fight. I can feel my mind thrashing, trying to figure out what to do, and then I realize.

My head is in chaos. My body is absolutely still.

Every ounce of my resistance flees. He's not being an asshole. He's giving my head the same kind of tie-down he's given the rest of me.

Drops of wax.

Chapter Forty-Five

ELI

Fuck, I almost pushed her too far and I don't even have her all the way tied up yet.

I want to wipe the sweat off my forehead, but that would involve taking my hands off the woman who has just utterly melted under my touch, and there's no way I'm letting go of what she just gave me. Spanking her ass was pure instinct, and for the rest of my natural Dom life, I will revisit the horror of the ten seconds afterward.

The ones where I thought I'd totally blown it—and where she decided to turn it into a gift instead.

I'm beginning to realize just how high this woman's expectations of her Dom are going to be. I reach for the wide straps I've rolled under the chaise lounge. I need to get us to the part where we're seeking her pleasure and not just her capitulation. A more experienced sub would know they're both coming, but if I get nothing else right today, I can't let myself forget how new she is.

Three knots, three bands. One around her hips, one around her ribs, one over her shoulders with her hands tucked inside for good measure. I won't add the last one that would normally be there. I saw her cast a careful, intrigued look at the wide band Tim used to restrain Mira's head during their wax play, but there are limits that even an idiot Dom shouldn't cross with a beginner, and that's one of them.

I am going to give her as much of a taste as I can. I collect up her hair, making sure it's clear of the leather straps, and form it in a loose knot on the back of her head. A quick twist into a hair tie and I've taken care of basic safety—and made sure I have a really clear view of her face. She might imagine I'll be watching elsewhere, and every so often I will, but this scene will live or die on what happens above Chloe's neck.

Another quick twist with a second hair tie and a repurposed nipple clamp and I have her head hooked in to the leather wrapping her arm. It won't hold her if she pulls very hard, but it will keep her head motion restricted unless she really needs to get it free.

The kind of restraint that only works if a sub wants it to work.

She makes an odd, gurgling sound in her throat as she tests to see what I've done, but I don't miss the bemused smile that comes after.

I lean down, running my hands over the leather bands. A cage, built to set her free. "Still comfortable?"

There's no fight this time. Just quiet acquiescence. "Yes."

There's no way that's the end of her fight, but I stroke her neck, her back. Taking a moment to soothe, to let her feel held by my leather, because soon my hands need to go elsewhere for a while. She hums, a low sound of pleasure that has some of the early notes of arousal I've been waiting for.

I grin and stand up. Time for my big gamble of the day, one sixteen-year-old Eli wouldn't have been wise enough to make.

It's time to take her to her cliff, and I'm not going to do it with my hands or with any of the kinky skills I've learned in the last twenty years. Because Quint was right—she doesn't trust those. Not yet.

I am, in the purest way I know, going to ask her to trust *me*.

Chapter Forty-Six

CHLOE

I hear him clanking around, making the kinds of noises a man or a small child makes when they're trying to be quiet. I let the amusement bubble in my belly a little.

The sounds quiet, and then his hand is on my back again, working its way up into my hair. I know I should be furious he tied my head still, but I feel like a newborn baby. Held. Freed from all responsibility. Getting me ready for the real work of today that will happen on the inside.

Because I don't think for a minute that the hard part of this is over.

Something slides behind my head, and then there's cool fabric resting on my forehead. "This is a blindfold, Chloe. You have your safewords."

I don't need a safeword for a little piece of cloth. Or so I think until it slides over my eyes and shuts off the world. I hear my breathing, harsh in my ears—and nothing else. I can't see, I can't move, I can't touch, and that little piece of cloth just put the camel's back under an avalanche of straw.

Eli's hand strokes my neck, my fingers, the line of my

spine. Soft, trailing touches that aren't trying to arouse, aren't trying to soothe—they're just there. A compass point in a dark, scary world.

He's there. He's got me.

And he's put me in this place of topsy-turvy blackness entirely on purpose.

I grit my teeth. I will get even. I asked him to push, not to smash me with a hammer.

I hear a chuckle, low and amused and moving away. He's not touching me anymore—and he clearly heard my threat as loudly as if I'd spoken it. Which is also new. Eli was always sensitive, but he used to wait until he had permission to eavesdrop on my soul.

My heartbeat pulses in my fingers, and I realize both my hands are fists. Which is a waste of energy, because even if he put his nose right up against my knuckles, I can't move enough to do any damage. I breathe, sending peace to my hands, and a promise that they will have their day. More breaths and my shoulders drop away from my ears, leaving quivering muscles in their wake.

I remember the woman on the table, under the wax. The way she tensed when her Dom tried to take her over the edge. And wonder if I've hit mine this soon.

More air in and out, trying to do what has never worked very well on a yoga mat, but I don't have a lot of other options. I'm a creature of sound and movement, and while I could probably deafen his neighbors from here, without being able to move that's just going to make me feel like a prisoner. A helpless one.

I feel my breathing start to shake. This is headed so very deep inside me and we've barely begun. Somehow, it's that embarrassment, that shame over my own weakness, that's driving me closest to breaking. I'm a woman who knows who she is and what she wants and what she can take, and this moment is challenging all three.

And the man who put me here has left me all alone.

Chapter Forty-Seven

ELI

I wait, bow poised over strings, cursing the well-developed Dom intuition that's keeping my hands still. Chloe is falling, and she's falling hard, but she's not quite there yet. She's still trying to fix this with anger, with comfort, with breaths that keep catching on the jagged edges of what she's grappling with.

We both had too many moments of helplessness in our childhoods, those awful voids as we got ripped away from roots and friends and home by the whims of the army and parents who tried to convince us it was all one big adventure. Chloe learned to adapt, to roll, to ride the wave.

Today I'm asking her to dive beneath it. To surrender. To let it hurt and to let it break her apart and to let me catch her out the other side.

But I saw her on that swing in Sam and Leo's back yard. I *know* her. If I offer solace too soon, she won't go under. I watch her face, listening to the sounds as her own breathing slowly tears her asunder. It's pure, unholy arrogance to think I can walk her through this, but I know I can. Not because of who I am. Two decades of kinky training is dandelion fluff in this moment.

This will work because of who she is—because of who she's always been. And because, somehow, the wonder of who she is has always been willing to let me step in close and be all of who I am.

I can hear the thickness in her inhales and exhales now, the incoming tears. The hard-ass in my head who has been shackling my hands finally lets them loose and I set bow to strings, giving the tears inside her sound and freedom and fury. It wasn't what I intended to play, but that doesn't matter.

My cello has just become Chloe's voice.

She freezes at the first note, a woman finally remembering she isn't alone in the dark. And then she breathes out, an audible letting go that is the first exhale of her body instead of her brain. My fingers trill a few bird notes, laughing along with her. Spilling out my relief.

She squirms like I've tickled her ribs.

I let the notes come as they will, veering from laughter to tears. Naming this as a place where both are sacred. Both are needed.

I watch, grateful and awed and honored, as she slowly relaxes. Her shoulders, her fists, her thighs, letting go of warrior readiness, of the need to protect and defend and hold intact. She lets the music of my hands tug on her, stretch her out into taffy, a shape that still holds together but is readying for something else.

Something that begins to taste of pleasure.

I grin, a potent mix of sixteen-year-old boy and pleased Dom and relieved man with a cello, as her pussy shows the first signs of getting hot and bothered, a wet sheen that teases my nose even though there's no way I can smell her arousal from this far away. I put my appreciation into my hands, letting her hear what my eyes see, what that does to my own glow of pleasure and the much more primal flow of blood to my cock.

Because now we can begin to walk together.

Chapter Forty-Eight

CHLOE

Music isn't supposed to be sexy.

I have no idea why that's the place my brain has decided to take its last stand, and it isn't one that makes sense, because even as a teenager, Eli knew how to put passion into his music. But this is something else. Something fierce and swelling that somehow still feels like it's laughing at itself, and wrapping that boldness and laughter around me like the very softest of silks.

More bands to hold me.

I don't bother testing the trusses again. I'm tied up until Eli decides I'm not, and every time I think of that it makes me mad and it makes me hot. Which the sexy music isn't helping, and I'm pretty sure Eli has lined himself up to have a really good view.

I groan quietly into my fist. I would have let him watch, but the fact that he hasn't asked, that he's simply taking, and that he set me up for this from the very first strap he wrapped around my wrist, has anger and fire and heat fusing together in my belly. It's so very clear that he has a plan and I'm just a reacting, lurching mess.

Nothing about that should be sexy, but it is.

The heat between my legs pulses in time with his bow, quick notes and long, slick ones. I am becoming his instrument. Instrument and audience both, and all I'm supposed to do is lie here and let it happen. I blink, or something deep inside me does, anyhow, bringing up vivid memories of sprawling on Eli's bunk bed as he played in the corner. I used to do that for hours, willing ears for everything from scales to original pieces he wrote in the deep dark of night and never played for anyone but me.

My mind melts.

This is just the grown-up version of Eli's bunk. I never resisted that—giving myself over to his music was easy, something I sought out on purpose because there was a place in the flow of sound where everything else stopped and I could just be.

I smile into the dark. He's reminding me that I already know how to do this. That the only things I really need to fight are my own expectations. The ones where I'm an equal, participating sexual partner, not one tied down to a chaise with her arousal on display and the rest of her very literally in the dark.

I hear my giggle, loud and bouncy in my head and twanging into his music with all the grace of a drunken elephant. And then I hear his reply. Amused notes that bounce right back at me and pretend that elephants are exactly what I'm supposed to be.

Chapter Forty-Nine

ELI

I could do this forever. Sit here and play and make music with the sounds of the woman who is slowly finding all the absurd edges of this theater that is my life and opening herself to why they exist.

But that kind of generosity deserves rewards I can't pull off with my hands on bow and strings, and I'm pretty sure there are a few other things I could do for the rest of forever too. I lean over to my phone, scroll down until I find what I need, and send a message to the speakers in the room. The contents of my new album, taking over for fingers that have somewhere else they need to be.

I see her jolt, taking in the change. Realizing it means she can no longer rest comfortable in knowing where I am.

I keep my chuckle quiet. Doms aren't supposed to be easily amused—it messes with the mystique. I turn up the volume of the music a little, masking my steps on the rug. I let her hear the creak of the footstool as I pull it closer and take a seat.

It doesn't take any more than that for Chloe to go utterly still.

Smart sub. Amazing, responsive, gorgeous sub. I trail a

finger down her spine. Slowly. Rebuilding the meditative space that will hold us for what comes next. Watching her skin tremble. Feeling her breathe into a touch no heavier than fairy dust.

I smile. I might have to get some candle lessons from Tim. In the meantime, I have a few things in my bag of tricks that should take us to more or less the same place. Ones that won't do it gently—because I promised.

The music wrapping around us has a hot, almost Latin flavor, and I decide to go with it. I pull out a tube of my favorite body lube and let a little warm on my fingers. Then I reach for her earlobe.

She jumps, both at the touch and at the cool wet of the lube.

I grin. That will change soon enough. I rub, finding the sensitive places behind her ear, down the slope of her neck. Waiting for the special ingredients in the lube to do their magic.

Her breathing responds first, rapidly followed by a squawk of protest as the heat blows away any lingering remnants of her musically induced coma. One day I'll let her stay in that space while I play with my bag of toys, but not this one. Today I'm not only trying to seduce her body—I'm also wooing her mind. I watch her carefully. For most people, this lube is all about heat and tingling. For some, it causes an unbearable itch, which is why my fingers are tracing her earlobe and the line of her neck instead of the slick wet of her pussy.

I'm close enough to smell her arousal now, and it's hell to be depriving myself.

I decide the lube is torturing her in all the right ways and trail a finger down her arm, rubbing some into the inside of her elbow. Connecting the dots, one erogenous zone to the next. She hisses as I make my way to the peekaboo curve of her breast, and I don't need to see her eyes to know what messages I would read there.

I follow her ribs to her spine and meander my way down. Mimicking Tim's path with the wax as well as I can given that I'm dealing with the back of my sub instead of her front. I have my reasons for that and they're mostly kindness, although Chloe might feel differently.

I dip my fingers into the enticing divot at the base of her spine. I know exactly the moment Chloe begins to suspect what comes next. Cymbals clash in her breath, and an erratic moan that tells me just how fraught this moment has become.

I keep my fingers where they are, not amping up the tension, but not backing off on it either. Letting her choose. And then I remember how new she is, and lean I forward to make that obvious. "You have your safewords, shorty." I use the nickname very intentionally. I want her to know she can trust me, even if she can't yet trust this.

Slowly, the cymbals ebb from her breath. She's not relaxed, exactly, and she's not at all certain she wants this trail of sensation going where I intend to take it, but she's chosen not to fight.

Yet.

Chapter Fifty

CHLOE

Someone once dared me to eat a whole bag of those little red cinnamon hearts—the really spicy ones. Right now my skin feels like Eli is using those to finger paint. Tingling that borders on fire. Heat that sneaks up and then makes very clear it's not going away anytime soon.

Which makes the current location of his fingers wildly uncomfortable for more than one reason. I'm a grown woman and I've tried anal play, but I didn't much like it. I don't get off on trying the forbidden—I like my sex to feel good. I wiggle my ass the tiny amount the restraints will allow, trying to let Eli know I don't want to go there.

He traces a light trail of heat into the top of the valley between my ass cheeks. All the wiggling does is make his line a little crooked.

I try to speak, but all that comes out is a croak. I clear my throat and try again. "I don't like this, Eli."

His finger keeps tracing.

Dammit, he said he wanted to know how I was feeling. "I've tried it before and it's not my thing."

He leans closer. "I don't care what you've tried before. I

care about how you feel right now. You can stop this if you want, or you can wipe your slate clean and give this a chance. Up to you."

I hear the words that say I have choices, but this feels like negotiating with a very large boulder. "If I give this a chance, my ass is going to tingle like fire for hours. That's hard to undo."

He chuckles. "Only about thirty minutes." The fingers at the top of my ass crack are suddenly colder. Wetter. "Choose, Chloe. You stop this or you take it."

The growl is out before I can stop it.

He doesn't say a word. He doesn't have to. The straps and the blindfold and the fingers ready to cinnamon heart some of my most sensitive skin are speaking for him.

I clear my throat, entirely ready to end this—and then I remember the woman on the table. The fight that hit her body when the first drops of wax splashed between her legs. And the look in her Dom's eyes as he watched her struggle, as he met her defiance and her resistance and gave her what she needed anyhow.

The safeword that almost left my lips sinks back down into the ooze. I know why he's doing this, and somehow, that's worth suffering for—even cinnamon hearts in my ass crack. He seems to know this, because his fingers are moving before the ripples in the ooze clear, dragging cool slime down onto skin that's trying really hard to run away and getting nowhere fast.

And then the heat hits. The burning tingle of instant sunburn, except this time it's not itchy and sweaty and heading into annoying. It's a hot, zippy jolt of pleasure funneling straight to my core. I hear the moan that leaves me, and I know he hears it, because his fingers move, circling down into the same tight cavern where the jolt has just gone.

One finger, and then two, invading with the cinnamon hearts that are now my very favorite thing, lighting me on fire in the best possible ways. I try to wiggle again, this time to ask for more, and groan in frustration when I don't get any further than before. I need to move. It's not about being equal anymore, about sharing in the work—it's about the absolute need pounding inside me and the satisfaction I know his fingers will give me if I can just freaking figure out how to move.

His hand lands on my ass again, sharp and stinging. "Be still. Take what I give you."

There is potent threat in his words, the kind that sends shivering quivers bolting over my skin. I hold my ass as still as I can and try to will his fingers deeper inside. He's toying with me, sliding a knuckle in and out, and I need more.

"Better." I get a little more penetration as a reward, and then I hear the bubbling squirt of the lube bottle just before I feel the cool, sticky mess that glops down my pussy. I wrinkle my nose at the ungainly delivery—and then I feel the heat. A tsunami of it, driven by his fingers straight into my slick folds.

The fingers in my ass plunge deeper as two more invade my pussy, plundering armies bearing hot, tingling lava. I strain against the ties that bind me, knowing I can't move, knowing he doesn't want me to, and entirely unable to stop.

Chapter Fifty-One
ELI

She's going to have bruises. I shake my head as Chloe strains against the straps, but the last thing she needs right now is for me to free her. She's so very close—to orgasm and to the lesson that lives beyond, if I can get her there in one piece.

Or a million pieces. I grin and curve the fingers in her pussy to catch her g-spot with a little more force.

She goes over before she even realizes she's going, one long shudder from her forehead to her toes. I tease out the aftershocks with both hands as she cries her pleasure into my once-boring living room.

I wait, stroking easily, the lube working its dastardly, fiery magic on my fingers as Chloe starts to soften. Which isn't anything I intend to let happen. I lightly stroke the rim of her back hole where most of her nerves live and run my other thumb over her slick clit. She convulses. "No, Eli—I need to stop."

I don't think she does. Not for a long time yet. "You have your safewords."

A long pause, and then an exquisitely frustrated gurgle.

I manage not to laugh out loud. Instead, I put my amusement into the parts of me that are strumming her clit.

The gurgle shifts to a long, liquid moan. I collect up the remnants of her first orgasm and throw them at the spiraling energies of the second. Three decades of fingering exercises have their upsides, and I use all of them to build the layers of her pleasure. This orgasm won't come quite as easily, and it shouldn't. I want her to go where I take her, not where her aroused body can practically take itself.

This time, when she comes, it's not an edge. It's a wave, one with soft, intense moans and the clenching of her pussy around my thumb. Which is sexy as fuck, and my cock is busy writing sonatas about why he needs a turn in there.

Soon.

Very soon. I slide my fingers out of her pussy and dedicate my whole focus to her ass. Whoever introduced her to anal play clearly did a lousy job, and the next time I dribble lube on her back hole I want the protest to be one of impatience, not lack of desire. I spread her ass cheeks with my fingers, using my thumbs to press the sides of her puckered hole. The skin is red and slick, nicely lubed, and gorgeously enticing.

I circle my thumbs, clockwise and counterclockwise, squeezing the delectable globes of her ass as my thumbs move. I build the pressure in my thumbs, keeping the angles so they press, but don't penetrate. This isn't an invasion. It's a seduction.

Her breathing shifts into soft little pants, her arousal trying to pull her somewhere her body isn't ready to go. No matter what the romance novels say, orgasm number three requires some serious effort, and I want it to be mine, not hers. I keep up my slow thumb torture until her breathing gets gorgeously ragged and her whole body becomes a lot more pliant.

She's learning.

I leave her ass to one thumb, pushing in up to the knuckle while my other hand heads back to her pussy. The sound she makes is dark and decadent, teetering right on the edge of surrender. She knows I can take her where she wants to go.

I tease around the edges of her clit, exploring the swollen folds, taking a few dips into her wet heat. She moans, equal parts pleasure and frustration, as I don't give her quite enough of any one thing to take her over. I keep teasing. Edging's not really my kink, but I'll hold her here as long as it takes, because the thing I want her to see is shimmering on the horizon, and be damned if I'm going to take it away from her with my impatience or hers.

A long, jagged breath and her pussy soaks my hand.

I blink, but she hasn't come—it's a different edge she's gone over.

The one where pleasure comes purely from the act of letting go.

Chloe just jumped off her cliff.

Thank fuck.

I run my fingers around her clit, steering clear of the over-sensitive tip and squeezing the sides. The thumb in her ass stays still, anchoring her surrender.

Chloe doesn't make any sound at all as she comes. She barely moves. She just sinks into the puddle of pleasure we've built together and lets herself dissolve.

I'm on my knees, cock out of my pants and poised at her entrance before her pussy stops fluttering. I stroke my hand down her back. "Stay exactly like that, sweetheart. I'm going to fuck you until neither of us can walk, and I want you to let me."

Words for the ears of a gorgeous newbie, even if she's gone deep enough she probably won't hear them until we're done.

I slide in, one hot fast stroke that nearly has me coming

inside her. I stop for a minute, warring with my cock for control of the bus while the lube does its damage to my sensitive parts, and let my finger play in her ass. Chloe doesn't move at all, which strokes my Dom ego almost as nicely as she just stroked my cock.

She's done fighting. Now I get to show her what lives out the other side.

Chapter Fifty-Two

CHLOE

I hear him saying things, but there's no blood left in my ears. Or my brain. I'm not sure I'm a person anymore. I'm primordial, pleasured goo, lying still and letting him carry me to the stars.

He plunges into me again and my brain tries to send all the necessary signals to my legs, to my hips, to the part of me where my spine once lived. Rise up, tilt, meet his thrusts, join in the crazed dance of mating his pleasure to mine.

Nothing moves. Nothing except the liquid reverberations of his cock into the lava of who I've become.

His legs shift against mine, and the next thrust blasts straight into nerves so sensitive it's a wonder time doesn't stop. He hammers short and deep, excavating things I didn't know were inside me. My clit is a never-ending scream of almost there, which makes no sense because it's already so far past anywhere it's ever been.

I'm pretty sure there are tears running down my face. And maybe snot.

Primordial goo.

My eyes have stopped straining against the blindfold. All I

need to see is right inside me. The dark that wraps around both of us, full of the primeval, slick joining of his fire to mine. The slapping sounds of his thighs, imposing separation and driving us back together.

My thighs are neither helping nor resisting. They just are. Two stacks of cells suffused with pleasure so intense and so deep that orgasm seems like a weak word for what's happening to me.

Something snaps on the back of my head, and it's suddenly free, cast adrift into the world with no direction. I hear my whimper. Lost.

His hand is there a moment later, his fingers running up the nape of my neck and taking hold in a way that flimsy ties never could.

He has me. All of me.

I hear his jagged breath making rough, intense, arrhythmic music with mine, and somehow that sets me alight, because I'm not alone in this place of fire and intense, beating need. Our sounds morph into something that isn't two anymore, feeding a glow that I can see, growing right at the very heart of us.

Something penetrates deep that isn't his cock, and the glow explodes into so many pieces that there is no longer any dark.

Chapter Fifty-Three

ELI

Kink lives or dies in aftercare.

I don't know whose words those are—I just know they're the first coherent ones I put together as my star-blown fragments fall slowly back to Earth. The most soul-shattering scene of my life, and I have no idea what it means. Where it will go. Who I will be when it ends.

I breathe into the hot, sweaty hair of the woman I'm mostly draped on top of and try to pull the fragments of who I am back together. I'm her Dom, and she's going to need me with my shit reassembled. I managed to get her untied and both of us to my bed before my muscles lost all coherence, but that's only the beginning of what I need to do.

I need her to see. Maybe she chooses this and maybe she doesn't, but I need her to understand the power and the brilliance of what we just did together.

I roll over onto my back, managing a grin at the Chloe limpet that sticks to me as I go. She totally doesn't have her bones back yet.

A floppy hand lifts up and ineffectually swats my chest. "Stop laughing, it's making you bumpy."

Or I think that's what she said. Her words sound six feet underwater. Maybe they are. I stroke gently down her back, feeling her sweat and the ridges my leather straps left in her skin. Those will fade quickly, even though I don't want them to. Evidence of what we made together. I finally get why some Doms don't like using healing gels to soothe the bruises.

She'll have some. Even the softest leather binds if you fight hard enough, and she did. Never in panic, though. Just resistance. Fear of being helpless. All leading to the beautiful moment when she realized that helpless is just a point of view and surrender holds all the power there is. Or at least I hope that's what she got from this.

I breathe in, trying to collect my words. I'm not usually a guy at a loss for them.

Her hand swats my chest again. "Stop thinking. Too loud."

I grin. I missed the years of hungover Chloe. I'll have to take surrender-drunk instead. "We need to talk. When you're ready."

Her grunt makes perfectly clear what she thinks of that suggestion.

If I let her fall asleep like this she'll be too stiff to get out of bed in the morning. I stroke a hand down her back again, this time using a little more pressure. Helping her spine to wake up. "Shower. Food. Then you can nap for as long as you want."

She somehow manages to lift her head up, pinning me with still-glazed eyes full of mutiny. "Red. Stop. You're not the boss of me."

This is probably not a good time to tell her just how sexy she is when she's pissed. My cock flexes against her leg, clearly disagreeing with me.

Chloe's eyes clear and she flops over on her back, chuckles rolling right up from her belly.

My cock is dumb enough not to understand she's laughing at him. He stands at attention, stupidly hopeful that this is a new form of foreplay. I send him a wry look. That would break all of us.

Chloe swats at my erection, missing by a mile, which is hopefully on purpose. And chuckles again.

I grin and snuggle in beside her. This is one way to bleed off all the spillover energy of a mind-blowing scene. Although if her breasts keep jiggling in that really pleasing way, more than my cock is going to forget that this is supposed to be the end. I reach over and touch one, just because I can.

This time she doesn't swat at me. She rolls back over and cuddles into my hand, laying her cheek on my shoulder and sliding a sweaty leg between mine.

I stroke her hair again. I saw her eyes clear. It's time to talk.

Not because she needs it. I do.

My skin is still on fire. All of it, even the parts I'm pretty sure Eli never smeared with cinnamon-heart lube. It's making it hard to concentrate on anything else. I want to just lie here and be happy embers, but I can hear his mind clinking.

He's always been a loud thinker.

I trace my fingers through the fuzz of dark hair on his chest. "What's churning in there, love?"

I feel his smile, and his regret. "I'm sorry. I'm trying not to go all cerebral on your afterglow."

Too late—and I've always gotten off on his brain too. I lift my head up and rest my chin on his chest. "That was amazing, but you know that." He's glowing plenty, even if he can't keep his brain quiet.

"It was." He strokes my cheek, his eyes holding a hint of melancholy. "Kink isn't always like that. It's powerful, and it can be really amazing, but that was..." He stops, clearly out of words.

It doesn't matter. I have them. "It was the most overwhelming sexual experience I've ever had." So deep it almost felt holy. I grin and make a face at him, because holy isn't where I want this to go. "What the heck is in that lube, anyhow?"

He chuckles, and some of the melancholy clears. "Dom secret."

I wrinkle my nose. "I joined the wrong team, did I?"

I see the seriousness land with both feet—and the compassion. The intention. Whatever just scared him serious, he clearly intends to take care of me first. He reaches out and strokes his thumb along the curve of my collarbone, the tenderness palpable. "I don't know that you've joined any team."

Ah, that's what's got him by the short hairs. I smile and stretch up to kiss his cheek. "You're composing, Eli. Listen to the damn music that's already playing."

His eyebrows fly up.

I grin. Surprising him is still fun. "Stop worrying about the labels. We know what we need to know."

He blinks. "Which is what, exactly?"

I wrap the words up like the sexy, careful, deeply intended gift that they are. "In what just happened—did you get what you needed?"

He nods slowly.

I smile and will him to hear my truth. "Do I look like a woman who had any scrap of what she needs go undelivered?"

The grin starts all the way down deep inside him—and then it stutters. "That might not be what you need tomorrow."

I hit his chest, and this time I have enough muscles back online to make it register.

He laughs. "The next time I tie you up, remind me that you're feisty when I set you free."

There we go. His soul just got there, even if his brain hasn't caught up yet. "Next time, huh?"

I watch as his brain and his soul collide—but not for long.

It's my turn to drive this thing. I lean in and kiss his cheek again. "Of course there will be a next time, silly. They might not always look like this, because I don't know how often I can do what I just did and be a functional human being who remembers how to speak. I might need space, or contrast, or a lesson on how to use your leather straps."

That makes his eyebrows do really funny things.

I don't care. We've got this, and I can see it, even if he can't. "Eli, my big fear was that I wouldn't be able to participate in your kinky world in any meaningful way. That would have been a deal breaker, an unworkable crack in our foundation, just like if I hated listening to your cello or you thought lingerie was for women who'd sold their self-worth to the devil."

His eyes are laughing, even as his arms reach to pull me in tighter. "You can dress up in sexy scraps of lace and listen to me play the cello any time you want."

I don't bother hitting his chest again—it seems to have very little effect. "Focus. Foundations. Cracks. The horrible fear that you lived in a world I couldn't understand or value or join."

His laughter flees. "Join is a big word."

I shake my head. I refuse to let this get hard. I already did my time there. "It doesn't have to be. Maybe I visit, maybe I move in, maybe I turn into Fettered's resident lingerie maven and let you tie me up one Thursday a month."

He raises a hand.

I snicker. "Fine. Every other Thursday."

He grazes his knuckles down the curve of my breast, somewhere in the vicinity of my heart. "You're saying we can figure this out."

I lean in and kiss his adorably confused lips. "Yes. I showed up, you pushed me, and something spectacular happened. The rest is negotiable, unless you get really unreasonable."

He laughs. "Most subs sit meekly in their Dom's laps for aftercare."

I don't do meekly very well. Especially after I've just done wondrously shattered. "I might need some latex pants for that part."

This time his laughter shakes the ceiling. "I'll ask Ari where she shops."

I smirk. The day I can't sew a pair of pants hasn't arrived yet. Although shopping for them with Eli in tow might be a lot of fun.

ELI

She's just tied me down and set me on fire at least as thoroughly as I did to her. And for the same reasons.

Respect. Generosity. Love.

I can let that last one out of its cage now. It might not be safe to love Chloe Virdani, but it's possible. The here-and-now version, and not the one tucked away into the very best parts of my history. We have as much chance at this as any two opinionated people in their forties who know how freaking precious this is.

Because it is, and we weren't wise enough at sixteen to know that. We let ourselves walk away because we didn't know that people who can see your soul and love it anyhow are damn hard to find, and they don't always come packaged together with a lifetime of sex appeal. We were smart enough to treasure each other, but we weren't ready to treasure what could be between us.

I feel so very ready now I want to leap out of my skin. Except for the part where I'm a lazy pile of boneless contentment. I have the woman watching me with an amused smirk on her face to thank for that. She's done what every good Dom sets out to do—she's shut down my head. I run my hand down her ribs, hoping what lives inside can feel my touch and my aching gratitude.

Her fingers slide up to join mine. "I want to listen to the music that was playing again. Sometime when you're not trying to drive me crazy."

That's an easy one. "You can have the live version if you want."

"Both." She grins. "I'm greedy, and there are a few parts that are kind of seared into my memory."

I lost track of the music by her second orgasm. "Like what?"

She hums a few bars that are an impressively good rendition of the bridge in a piece that is all about thunder and lightning and what happens after the rain. It's also the last track of the album. Her ears should have been hopeless goo at that point. "I can't believe you heard that well enough to remember it." I shake my head into her hair. "You were supposed to be thoroughly distracted by then."

"Of course I was listening. The music is you." She smiles into my shoulder. "Those bars are when my hair tie broke."

The accident that gave me a chance to run my fingers into her hair and hold us both as the storm arrived. I hum the bars quietly again, touched right down to my bones. She held my music that tightly, even as she shattered.

Respect. Generosity. Love.

I pick up the blindfold lying on the edge of the bed and scrunch it into my fist. It's going straight into my new gear bag. The one put together with a certain lady in a sexy red dress in mind.

Chloe wraps her fingers around my closed hand. "That was mean, I'll have you know. And it's a poor design."

I chuckle. "I imagine you can fix that."

She fingers the elastic, hanging down between my fingers. "I might. Or I might keep this one." She lifts her head up, pinning me with a look I'm very quickly beginning to recognize. The eye-gaze version of latex pants. "Don't get rid of it. Or the chaise. I'm oddly fond of both of them, even if they're badly made for the job."

The chaise wasn't remotely made for what I just used it for. "And the body lube?"

She raises a stern eyebrow. "That can go."

I touch my finger to the tip of her nose. "Yes, ma'am."

She snorts as I trace a path all the way down to her pussy. "Troublemaker."

I let a couple of my fingers take a dive into the mess we've left there. "Maybe we should give the body lube one last hurrah before we wash it off forever."

She rolls onto her back, giggling like a teenager. "You break me, you have to keep me."

I grin. I intend to—and I love that she's leaving the choice of what happens next up to me. Setting down the reins, letting her Dom pick them back up. I slide my fingers out of her pussy and back up to her belly. Power exchange with Chloe is always going to be heavy on the exchange part. She'll need it to balance her wild surrender.

Which is fine by me. I'll buy her all the latex pants she wants, as long as I'm the one who gets to peel them off her.

I stroke my hands over skin sticky with sweat and lube. I don't want to let even that go. It's part of the shape and texture of this moment, and I'm not done collecting all the notes.

Because I'm absolutely collecting them. This will head to my cello soon. It's the only place I know other than a scene to lay down all of who I am, and this deserves to be memorialized.

The afternoon I met the rest of my life.

Chapter Fifty-Six
ELI - EPILOGUE

It's the same woman, in the same red dress, waltzing into my club and making my fingers fumble. I shake my head and try to pick back up before I send the band totally off the rails. We have a big audience tonight, and I suspect the vixen who just walked in the door knows that.

Chloe scans her audience, a sexy queen accepting her dues.

She strolls toward me slowly, casually meeting my eyes as she scans the room, but nothing more. Which makes me want to leap off the stage and grab her. Quint smirks in my direction, but I ignore him. I've seen him dance to his barmaid's tune often enough.

Scorpio hits the kind of chords that say she's changing songs and already told me once, and I shake my head, trying to get the Chloe fog out from between my ears. The lounge laughs, right on cue. Funny Dom.

Dom who had hot, sweaty sex with the vixen in red less than three hours ago and still can't think straight.

Jackson's drums are clearly snickering at me, but I don't care. I throw a jazzy riff into whatever we're playing and manage not to pump my fists when Chloe grins. She might not be looking, but I've learned just how sensitive she is to the right music. One day soon I'm going to have to figure out how to play my cello with my feet. Until then, the recorded stuff will have to do.

Although my hands happen to be available right now.

This time, it's me who grins. I play a cut-off for the band. When they crash into silence, I play a single note. Repeat it. Follow it up with three more, a climbing minor chord. It doesn't have quite the timber it does on my cello, but it doesn't matter.

Those notes are a direct line to Chloe's heart.

Her entire body softens as she comes to a stop, staring up at me with the kind of look that heads straight into my fingers and sends them soaring. I play my heart back to her in the notes I wrote before I knew she was coming back into my life. Thunder and lightning and the soft rain after the storm.

She will, always and forever, be my soft rain.

Jackson has picked up some kind of quiet, funky rhythm that mimics raindrops down to the ground, and I can see Scorpio and Quint noodling with their fingerboards, trying to find the key to join in. Our audience is murmuring, swaying with the kind of romantic, swooning energy that could only happen at a kink club.

I smile at Chloe, drinking in the easy contentment and the rushing joy of this scene she's just landed us in. The sexy ones are my domain. Everywhere else, it's fun to let her play. Especially when I can leak her brain out her ears with just a few notes. I ad lib a bridge and swing back around to the beginning of the piece. Quint and Scorpio come in right on cue, tracing the lines of a melody they've only heard once.

Once is enough for musicians of their caliber, especially ones who know what it is to be the lightning and the rain.

Quint could probably use this song as a membership test. It's kinky down to its very last note.

I let the music roll over me, as it's meant to. And in the center of its swell, I put my heart out into the universe and ask Chloe to see. Her eyes close. She does that often these days. A blindfold of choice. Touching our love at its deepest roots.

I'm working on a new piece. It's called "Love is Strongest in the Dark".

My fingers reach the final bars of the section I've just taught the band how to play. I'll bring the whole thing to practice when we're not holding the hearts of half the lounge in our hands. I let the final notes die out, never taking my eyes off the woman who has walked into far more than my club.

And then I rap out a bunch of quick chords that belong to one of our standards—a raucous rock 'n' roll cover I can play on autopilot.

Because there is naked truth here tonight—but there is also theater.

Chloe throws back her head and laughs, which turns my cock to steel and demolishes the rest of me. Her head snaps up, and the regal queen is back—along with eyes that say she's not nearly done messing with me yet.

I hammer a few chords that won't do the song any harm. Game on, shorty.

Chloe strolls up the three low steps to the stage, an elegant strut that only a woman entirely at home in her sexy skin could pull off. The theater training probably doesn't hurt, either.

My fingers are still playing, but I have no idea if they're even in the vicinity of the right song. She takes my breath away and scrambles my brains and a whole lot of other parts of my body further south.

Because she will also, always and forever, be my thunder and lightning.

Chapter Fifty-Seven

CHLOE - EPILOGUE

He knows so very much about who I am and what I need. Aching softness and playful fire. Balance.

He doesn't need to ask twice.

I roll my hips as I close the distance to the sexy man behind the keyboard, sending my dress shimmying in a way that should make at least a few people drool. I only care about one, and the hot appreciation in his eyes is fuel for the fire of everything I am.

Which doesn't mean I intend to go down easy.

I pause beside him, hands on my hips, and strike a pose. Then I lean in, breasts on display right in front of his eyes, and run a light finger around the back of his ear. "Well hello, sexy."

I know he's the only one who can hear me, but the audience laughs anyhow, willing to go along with whatever joke I've got lined up.

I raise an eyebrow at Scorpio as the musical volume suddenly dims. She shrugs a shoulder at Ari, who's standing by the sound system.

I grin. It's always good to have accomplices.

I speak again into the space that's suddenly not full of earsplitting sound. "I heard you were playing tonight. Thought I'd come listen." I slide smoothly into Eli's lap, with an extra wiggle for the delightfully hard cock waiting for me there. I wrap an arm around his shoulders and kiss his cheek. "Don't let me get in the way."

Our audience hoots and hollers like they're meant to—the subs because it's always good when someone else is at the front of the troublemaker line, and the Doms because they fully expect Eli will get even.

Just in case he hasn't figured that one out, there are helpful suggestions from the crowd. The loudest is a voice I recognize. "You need to work on your sub's manners, Eli." Harlan tips his head at me and grins. He knows exactly what he's doing.

Scorpio gives him a look that could strip paint off a rocket, which just causes more hooting and hollering. I notice that nobody bothers to give him suggestions. I grin his way. "I have a couple of special pieces set aside at my store you might like."

Harlan looks interested. Scorpio looks ready to kill, and I'm at the very top of her list. I run a sexy hand down Eli's chest. "Lace is a nice look for a cock, don't you think?"

Scorpio doubles over laughing, which probably means I won't get stabbed tonight.

Eli growls in my ear, but he's far too amused to be taken seriously. And far too aroused. I grind into the hardness pushing up into parts of me that are already getting expectantly slick.

Eli palms a breast with one hand and fists my hair with the other.

I whimper. That's my kryptonite and he knows it.

He speaks loudly enough for the audience hanging on our every word. "Do you know what happens to subs who interrupt their Doms, shorty?"

Some wisecracker in the audience pipes up. "Is that what she's named your cock, Eli?"

I'm smart enough not to laugh, but Quint isn't. Eli plays the opening bars to *Rocky* one-handed on his keyboard and the man on second guitar manages to quiet himself. Mostly.

Jackson, in an act both brave and stupid, picks up the *Rocky* beat.

Eli switches to the theme from *Star Wars*.

I shake my head and pick up his hand, plunking it back on my breast. "Focus, Sir."

He growls, even though I can feel his ribs shaking. "There must be some kind of impact play you haven't made a hard limit."

We've never had a formal discussion about that, but I know my man. "Any kind that lands on your ass is just fine, Sir."

The shaking in his ribs gets perilously close to a seizure. "I'm thinking it's time for you to learn to play the keyboard, sweetheart."

That's totally not in the script, but Eli has always been good at improv. I helpfully place my hands on the keys.

He wraps his arms around mine and plays the opening bars to "These are a Few of my Favorite Things." Which happens to be literally the only song I know how to play, courtesy of a really awful stint skipping through the theatric hills of high school as a music-loving nun.

I wince. "I'm not sure that's a really appropriate song for the club, Sir."

I hear his evil grin, even though I can't see it. "Oh, I'm sure our audience can help you with some new words."

The audience suggestions ramp up to outrageous in two seconds flat. I ignore them. There's no way he's done. Eli's evil comes in layers.

His cock grinds up into my ass crack, and his next words are full of Dom glee. "You might want to get started. You don't get to come until you have three verses with club-appropriate lyrics."

I squirm as he gives my nipple the kind of tweak that makes my clit sing. "Do they have to rhyme, Sir?"

He chuckles as his hand moves to my other breast. "They do now."

I lean into his fingers, needing the touch, even if it will make me crazy. "You're going to make me regret this, aren't you?"

His next words are quiet and heartfelt and meant just for me. "No, shorty. Not ever."

Chapter Fifty-Eight

CHLOE

I hold up the pants and make a face at Ari. "The quality of these is total garbage."

She snickers. "I know. Which is why you're making my next pair, but first you need to get the vibe, so we're here playing dress-up. Quit looking under the covers."

It's an occupational hazard, but she has arranged for us to be here at the crack of dawn when no other self-respecting people in latex are awake. Which lets me poke and prod at things without some worried shopkeeper breathing down my neck.

Yes, I recognize the irony.

Ari scoops up a vinyl bustier that looks like it might crack if I breathe too hard, a pair of pants that match, and a neck collar that actually looks fairly well made. She eyes my feet and heads for the boots in the corner. "Size?"

Seven, although I'm pretty sure it won't matter. My ankles feel broken just looking at the display rack. When you aren't very big, you have to own your size, not strap five-inch heels on the bottom. That's just a good way to get a nosebleed. I walk up beside her and take down the pair least likely to cause me permanent brain damage. "Anything else before I head in there and try to sausage myself into those pants?"

She grins. "Everyone needs to have the sausage experience at least once."

Not my clients. "I started making lingerie so I'd never have to do this again."

Ari giggles. "You're really grumpy before you've had coffee."

"Yes, she is," says a dry voice from behind us.

I turn, dragged around by the scent as much as the sexy man holding the coffee cups. "You're my hero."

He chuckles and hands one over. "That's not what you said last night."

I roll my eyes. Last night he proved just how much of a sadist he can be with nothing but feathers and an innocent looking glove.

He neglected to mention that the glove had teeth. Thousands of them, pinpoint sharp. Dom sandpaper. My skin might never be the same again, which will make the whole sausage process this morning even less fun than usual.

I pick up the pile of vinyl one-handed, cradling my precious coffee in the other. "I'll be out in a minute."

Ari strikes a pose that has Domme written all over it. "If you don't come out, I'm coming in to get you."

Eli grins. "I'll follow her in to watch."

I shake my head. Morning brings out my inner grump. It brings out Eli's immature delinquent. Who, I have to admit, my inner grump kind of enjoys.

Ari swings into a chair that's padded in the same cheap vinyl as the items in my hand. "Pro tip, put the pants on before the boots."

That doesn't deserve an answer. I swing into the tiny excuse for a dressing room, having fun despite myself. I don't get to play the grump with people who thoroughly don't care and find me amusing very often. If I pulled this stunt with Mandy, she'd have heart palpitations for a week. I take a huge swig of coffee, gird my loins, and stick one foot into the pants. Which plants me headfirst into the wall. Vinyl doesn't slide. At all.

"Oh, yeah." Ari's voice is laced with schoolgirl giggles. "Also, sit down before you put the pants on."

I take another swig of coffee. "The next corset I make for you is going to have strangulation ties." I'm not exactly sure what those are, but they sound dire.

"Nope." She sounds totally unconcerned. "Breath play is a hard limit."

Threatening Ari is like trying to convince rain it's scared of getting wet. "I'll make it puke green and festooned with polka dots."

This time it's Eli who laughs. "That one landed. Nice one, shorty."

My main cheerleader. I look at the pants, now mostly slicked on, in disgust. "I'm not coming out in these."

Ari sticks her head through the dressing room curtain. "Nice bra. Now you see the issues with the pants, yeah?" Eli's head pops in above hers. He takes one look at the pants and makes a face.

I wiggle my sausage-shaped ass his way. "Want me, darling?"

He doesn't even pause. "Yes."

I shake my head at their reflected grins in the mirror.

Chapter Fifty-Nine

ELI

The pants are hideous, but I don't care. The glint of fun in Chloe's eyes is worth every bit of what I had to give up this morning.

She doesn't bother trying to kick either of us out. She runs her hands over the pants instead. "I saw the issues before I did the sausage dance. Poorly sized, no give, and the cut is styled after a prepubescent boy."

"Exactly." Ari nods and hands in another pair. "These are the high-end, latex version. They're not quite so awful."

Chloe's hands are testing and tugging. "The cut is better, and the latex has some stretch, but not enough." She looks at Ari. "There has to be a blend available that will give the look of latex with the give to flatter more figures."

Ari sits on the tiny shelf that's probably meant to be a bench and steals Chloe's coffee. "You're the expert."

I love this. Watching Chloe be all of who she is, listening to that avid, curious brain of hers figuring out how to make instruments of quality for those of us who will appreciate them. Sharing who she is with one of my favorite people.

One who is quietly lonely. I can see it, here in the early

morning dim. Ari is throwing all of herself into appreciating who we are—and silently hoping she doesn't have to wait until her forties to find the same kind of belonging. I want to ruffle her hair and make her promises, but neither one would be at all respectful of the amazing person she is.

Chloe and I will just have to keep being living proof of what's possible, because the two women currently hamming it up in the changing room are peas from the same pod and they know it. I shift my gaze back to the shop, because if I sit here with compassion in my eyes for much longer, Ari will notice. My eyes land on the really bad collection of crops hanging in the window that I noticed on our way in.

The ones Ari told me not to judge. Poor students and hip, broke artists deserve kinky toys too.

I'm grateful I can afford the instruments I want these days.

Chloe has the offending vinyl pants off and the latex ones most of the way on, which is giving me a really nice show of her lace-clad ass. She definitely doesn't look like a sausage in these, although given her thoughtful frown, she's still not very happy.

She tugs on the waistband and makes a face at Ari. "These aren't awful."

"They're the best of the easily available ones in town." Ari has her business face on now. I stay in the shadows of the curtain and watch two pros at work. "Anything else I have to order online."

Chloe's already shaking her head. I know what she thinks about online retail. Fantastic for cat food, piss-poor for items that are meant to be a sensory, evocative experience. I can't disagree. It's the difference between canned music and live, and much as I hope to make my new living from the former, nothing will ever replace being able to speak straight to my audience's ears.

I chuckle and mentally take it back. Some things replace it very nicely.

Chloe casts me a knowing look and shimmies more than she needs to in order to slide out of her bra.

Ari claps her hands over her eyes. "Not looking."

Chloe laughs. "My boobs aren't that bad, oh young and perky one."

Ari groans. "It's not that. It's the look on Eli's face."

The entire universe, figuring out that a clown lives inside my sub. I reach out and tweak Chloe's nipple. "Behave, woman."

She snickers and reaches for a shiny black corset, which is probably an answer all by itself. I lean against the doorframe of the changing room and wonder just how many Doms have watched their subs put on dominatrix gear.

Chloe examines the lines of the corset in the mirror as she laces it up, but Ari is watching me. A switch on a mission, ready to jump into protective mode if her friend needs it. Which is totally unnecessary, but it warms me anyhow. Kink is always better with good friends in it.

I stick my tongue out at Ari, just in case she's coffee deprived enough to miss the message, and step in to help Chloe with the lacing. Also totally unnecessary, but I've never needed much excuse to put hands on her skin.

Her lips quirk as I neatly tighten the lacings. "You're pretty good at that."

I keep my attention on my fingers. "I am. Pretty good at undoing them too."

Ari bolts for the door, hands back over her eyes. "Not looking!"

Chloe's bubbling laughter is the high point of my morning.

Although what's about to happen next might give it some pretty stiff competition.

———

Preorder NEED, the final book of the Fettered series! Ari has been waiting so long... and now it's time.

(If you can't follow a link from here, go to liliamoon.com and I'll get you hooked up.)

xoxo Lilia

And don't worry, I have no plans to stop writing when this series is finished. I've already started work on the next one. Remember the rope-bondage guy Chloe saw in the dungeon? He's about to go on a road trip to pick himself up some very special handmade rope. *Twisted Strands*, book one of the Handcrafted trilogy, coming soon!

Made in the USA
San Bernardino, CA
23 February 2018